DATE DUE

The Eyes of Van Gogh

The Eyes of Van Gogh

CATHRYN CLINTON

CANDLEWICK PRESS
CAMBRIDGE, MASSACHUSETTS

To Amy Ehrlich, editor and friend, for caring about
and believing in both Jude and me

To all those who were in the Penn State Hershey Medical Center
Adult Outpatient Program, 3/3/1999 to 3/24/1999
Thanks for your belief in me. I continue to pray
that you are all alive and thriving.

First edition 2007

Library of Congress Cataloging-in-Publication Data
Clinton, Cathryn.
The Eyes of Van Gogh / Cathryn Clinton. — 1st ed.
p.   cm.
Summary: After many moves with her peripatetic mother, seventeen-year-old Jude
begins to believe that she has finally found a home, friends, and some purpose in life
when the grandmother she never knew has a stroke and she and her mother
come to live in the same town to be near her.
ISBN 978-0-7636-2245-9
[1. Self-perception—Fiction. 2. Artists—Fiction. 3. Friendship—Fiction.
4. Family problems—Fiction. 5. Coming of age—Fiction.
6. Gogh, Vincent van, 1820–1888—Fiction.]   I. Title.
PZ7.C622815Eye 2007
[Fic]—dc22   2006051840

2 4 6 8 10 9 7 5 3 1

Printed in the United States of America

This book was typeset in Plantin Light.

Candlewick Press
2067 Massachusetts Avenue
Cambridge, Massachusetts 02140

visit us at www.candlewick.com

PROLOGUE

A noise registered deep inside
the void that housed my mind.
It was the whoosh click *of a machine.*
Through the crack of one eye, I saw
the blinking red lights of the machine.
I'm still alive, *I thought,*
and then I sank
down,

down.

One

I hate the first day of school. I always have, but then nine new schools in thirteen years can do that to you. By second grade I was in my third new school, and that doesn't include the day cares.

I read somewhere that the average American family moves every three years. That makes me above average, but somehow it doesn't make me feel superior at all.

I walked home that first day. I'd decided not to ride the bus. I didn't live that far from the high school, and by the end of any school day I've had enough of people. So when a boy yelled at me out the window of a school bus that drove by, I ignored him, didn't even look. The chocolate smell from the factory in town surrounded me.

It was hot and humid, and little flyaway pieces of my hair stuck to my temples. I wanted to chop off my waist-length hair and looked into the window of a beauty shop as I walked by, but I withstood temptation. My hair's a trademark. The length doesn't change, only the color, and I liked the new black. It would wash out in a week. I had pulled it up on top of my head in a ponytail.

I didn't stop at our current abode that day. I needed to walk more. Walk from the dumb pain that had snaked into my brain again.

Pain and sadness are homeless beggars in my life, displaced feelings that come and go, plopping down for their own reasons, sleeping in any corner of my brain. They wear at me with a constant tiredness that I have to chase out.

Sometimes, though, a trigger pulls inside me, and the pain goes off, getting bad. It isn't like I know all the triggers, but school newness is a definite. Slamming lockers, cracked blinking fluorescent lights, whispery voices, self-conscious laughter, and a hundred elbows and shoulders bumping me, jabbing me, erasing me. It was as if I wasn't even there, and I wasn't, to them.

I walked up my street, through the square, past

the bar and the mill to the far edge of town. Along the railroad tracks, right by a signal light, I waited for the train to come in. I'd found this special place two weeks before. I bent down and touched the rail, listening. I was a little early.

I whistled as I walked along the tracks. I wondered if I could get off in time. I craved the rush that split my gut the moment the train vibrations began, and then the wave of utter control. *I* decided when to move.

There was a skittering sound above me and I looked up, knowing it was a robin, but I couldn't spot it. All I saw was a crow. It was watching me. When I looked down, I saw the blinking lights of the freight-train engine. It came toward me, coming slower and slower until it stopped.

Those lights looked like eyes, red-rimmed ones. I stared into the eyes. **Maybe it would be better if you weren't here.** That thought popped into my brain a lot. It is funny how words can appear in your mind even when you haven't thought them.

The tension left me as I stared at the train eyes, and my body relaxed. Focus does that. It blanks me out, no feelings, no pain.

Suddenly I felt the creative energy. I love it. It's so big, so limitless. When it hits me, I escape to my free-flow drawing world.

I live in the pencil, the paper, the object that I see gliding from my mind to my hands. It's a way of seeing that's mine, my way of defining a world. It's also a place to live when things are too dismal, too inferior, too tiring—or even too shining, too good.

I have a box with some drawings, notebooks, paintings, and sketchbooks that goes all the way back to kindergarten. That box has made all the moves. I colored on it in green crayon so I'd know which one it was.

When I was really little, my mom would pick it up, and say, "Go ahead. Climb in, Judith." She'd put it on my lap in the car. "This way we know we'll have enough room for it. You take care of it." I'd smile up at her. She knew it was important. Who knows how many thousands of miles that box sat on my lap.

There was a huge rock formation up behind the signal light. It looked like some smaller rocks piled on top of other bigger ones. Trees were actually growing on and in the rocks, snaking their roots down. Moss had settled on the rocks, the roots. I looked at it and thought, *Someday, I'll climb up and sit on the top rock,* but that day I stopped halfway up, where there was a little ledge I could sit on. I leaned back against the stone, pulled out my sketchbook, and began to draw.

I drew myself in a field. There were stars in the wavy weeds, stars in the trees, and in my outstretched hand was a star. A star with a tail. I stopped drawing and stared out at the sky, so blue between the trees. Was there a cosmic world, so timeless and other? Where people actually held stars in their hands?

The wind gusted and tugged at the paper. I dated it, like I do all my sketches, and I closed the sketch-book. I can trace my days by my sketches, with their dated moment markers. I put the sketchbook back in my backpack and left.

Hot pizza grabbed my nose when I hit Main Street. I glanced behind me and saw that someone had opened the door to the Brother's pizza place. I looked up and down the street and ran across, avoiding the traffic and the pizza. For such a small town, Ellenville, or E-ville as people around here say, has a lot of pizza places.

After school the next day, I walked up to the railroad track, then went to see my grandmother. My grand-mother was the reason we had moved to this town. A neighbor of hers sent my mother a letter letting her know that my grandmother had suffered a stroke and been put in a nursing home and that someone should come take care of her affairs. The letter had at least two change-of-address stickers layered on top of the original address, so it had taken a while to reach us. I was surprised that the neighbor had any address for us at all. We didn't get letters from my grandmother. I hadn't even known she was alive. Then the letter came and I had family. Was this just a blink in our roving life? Or dared I hope for more—like, say, HOME.

I'd kissed the letter and stuck it in my box. My grandmother would be home for me; I just knew it, even though Stella, my mother, had never talked about her.

Stella must have been enough when I was little, because I don't remember it being all bad, but the intervening years had weighed in heavily. Moving, moving to find the man, and then there was the drinking that had gone with each move. It was the same endless swirl down the sink of life.

Classic rock songs inspired the destinations of all our moves. The song about Memphis by Marc Cohn was one of Stella's favorites. We moved to Memphis when I was nine. As we drove there that summer, we heard it three times on the radio. Stella said it was a sign of good things to come. When the song came on, she turned it up full blast, rolled down the windows, and we sang along and car-danced. Stella is a good dancer, even sitting down.

On that trip she let me buy wads of grape gum and blue Slurpees at every gas station that had a machine. My tongue was a permanent blue, and I showed it to every driver that passed us. My mom just laughed at people's responses. She was too busy pumping her arm up and down to get the trucks to honk to worry about road rage. Good things didn't come in Memphis, and I started thinking that no matter where we moved, they wouldn't. Whenever I heard the song, I filled up with Memphis memory, Memphis sadness.

When we got the letter about Gram, we left Miami, where we were living at the time. The Miami move was inspired by Jimmy Buffett's song "Margaritaville." It was as close as we got to the Keys. Since all our previous moves were determined by songs, this Ellenville move was different, or so I thought.

This move was family, not bad boyfriends, bad jobs, or bad whatever. I'd always wanted more family, something more than Stella. It seemed to me that people with two good parents, grandparents, aunts and uncles, cousins had more of a chance in life. You have a place to come back to, and people for good times like birthdays, or for bad times like a broken arm or your mother getting fired.

Who could blame me for wanting things to be different? With each move Stella got more desperate, like a Jackie Chan cat being put in smaller and smaller cardboard boxes. She just chopped and kick-boxed bigger holes in each place.

The other thing I wanted was answers. Home was a place, a people, a history—good or bad—that told your story, and I wanted to know about Stella and me. I wanted to know about where I came from. I'd never find out from Stella. Could anything have lasted longer than her silence about the past?

But when we got to E-ville, my grandmother couldn't talk. The stroke had taken care of that. When I saw her in the Care Home that first time, staring and unmoving, my stomach muscles contorted so bad I couldn't stand.

Disappointment tastes like vomit. Maybe they are the same thing. It left me feeling like a night of dry heaves.

The stroke was more real than my grandmother, and I couldn't believe it. I could see it, touch it, and even understand it, but I couldn't do the same with my grandmother. When I got over the shakes, I looked up and she was still there. All the grandmother I'd ever have.

Stella stared at my grandmother and folded her arms across her chest. The lines around her eyes and the big one in her forehead smoothed out for the briefest moment. I knew that look. It was the "See?" look, the one she got when she thought she'd been proved right. Maybe she was settling up something from long ago. I didn't know for sure, because she was quiet.

Stella talks a lot. She has opinions on everything

and doesn't hesitate to say them without listening to anyone else's reply. It's only the past she doesn't talk about. That's gone and to hell with it, she'd say. Move on.

Stella smiled and nodded and then she left the room. I thought it was some sort of good-bye, but if it was, she didn't say it out loud to Gram or me. She never said a word about her visit, and she never went back.

Stella said she'd take care of Gram's stuff, and that left me to care for my grandmother. The owner of Gram's apartment had moved everything into a dilapidated garage out back. I didn't know what he would have done with the stuff if we hadn't shown up. Stella went through it in a frenzy, tossing out nearly everything. She saved some furniture for our apartment.

I saved one picture of a woman, a child, and an old man and put it in my grandmother's room at the home. Maybe the child had been my mother.

As I went into the Care Home, I wondered who had given it that name. Had anyone ever thought of it as caring or a home?

The air in the dark hallway, stale mold with a faint touch of disinfectant, blew across my face as I walked into my grandmother's room.

It was green, institutional green, like the color of bathroom walls in old buildings. I crossed to the bed where my grandmother lay. She looked the same. Her right eyelid drooped, and the rest of that side of her face sagged. Her hand lay in an exact clawlike curve on top of the blanket. Her other eye was open and staring. Was it hazel-colored like mine? It was hard to tell with all of the red veins in it.

I leaned over and kissed my grandmother on the cheek, right below the unblinking eye. This had taken some getting used to, because that eye looked a little scary.

I'd heard that people in comas could hear you. Some coma victims came out of it and could even tell you what they'd heard and thought. Maybe the same was true for stroke victims who couldn't talk; they could hear you and even communicate somehow. So I spoke to her, and she answered in my mind.

"I love you, Gram," I said. I waited for her to say the things I'd always wanted to hear.

She didn't disappoint me. *I love you too, sweetheart.*

"What can I do for you today?" I asked.

Tell me all about your day, honey. It's lonely here without you.

So I said, "Okay," and started the daily routine I'd made up for my visits with her.

I straightened the white cover and carefully tucked everything in. "Ms. Dennis, the art teacher at school, says that we have to do a research paper on an artist. I thought about Rodin, because I love *The Thinker*. But I decided that was too cerebral. Then I thought about Monet, but flowery just doesn't do it for me. Now I'm thinking about van Gogh, but I'm not sure. He painted my favorite picture, *The Starry Night*. It's pinned on my wall. It is so concentrated and mystical at the same time. The real picture is in a museum in New York City."

Perhaps we'll go together to see his painting someday. Truthfully, I love the drawings you've put up in here. You've got talent, girl.

It's sort of kindergarten to put your drawings up in someone's room, but I wanted my grandmother to know me. We had a lot of years to catch up on. There was a painting from my last day care, the "family pictures" of two stick people with large round hands and heads, and then a couple of grade-school pictures. The first one had a yellow sky, green ocean, and a rainbow with pink and black in it. The other one was an experiment with black and stars. There were the junior-high pictures of iguanas and ferrets, two pets I was sure I wanted but didn't think I'd ever get, and finally there were some drawings from my high-school sketchbooks.

I walked over to the window ledge. I hummed "Hey Jude," my favorite song. "Time to look at your plants."

Thank you. You take such good care of them. I watered the plants I'd brought in. They were all African violets—purple, pink, white, double-bloomed and ruffled. There was a different plant for each day of the week. The ledge was full.

As I checked for dead leaves and flowers, I said, "I know that van Gogh was sort of crazy and cut off his ear. Melissa, my friend in Ohio, used to cut herself too, and she was sort of artistic. Maybe they go together, craziness and art. What do you think?"

Oh, I don't think so, but it is an interesting thought. I mean you are artistic, Jude, and you aren't crazy. I started humming "Here Comes the Sun."

I turned to the sink and cleaned it with the cleanser I'd brought in. "I do know that his paintings sell for a phenomenal amount of money, but I think he was poor, so that's a mystery. I love mysteries, don't you?"

Yes, I do. That's something we have in common, good mysteries. I read so many when I was younger.

I swept the floor. When I finished, I went around the room, straightening the vinyl chair, the tray table, and each pleat of the dark green curtains. I was humming "Penny Lane." I stopped by the bed and squeezed my grandmother's uncurled hand. There was no response. I said, "Be back tomorrow. Love you."

I'll be waiting. I love you too.

I picked up my backpack and headed for the apartment. It was one of the upstairs apartments in an old two-story building. The building was yellow stone above red brick, separated by a slash of beige wood. The apartment was full of beat-up furniture that used to belong to my grandmother. Below the apartments was an abandoned drugstore. The building was on one of the main streets close to the town square, not far from the H&R Block office.

I was hoping Stella would be gone. Usually she was on her way somewhere or sleeping or drunk, depending on the time of day and her work schedule. When I was in kindergarten, she used to kiss me when I got home from school, but our kissing days were long gone. I ran up the stairs to the apartment, accidentally kicking off a large chunk of peeling gray paint and leaving a thick black scuff mark in its place.

I opened the door, took a deep breath, and went inside. Stella was there, and she was in a mood, screaming, throwing, and yanking. Spider-Man, my cat, was right inside the door, and he wrapped himself around my leg. Probably trying to get as far from Stella as he could.

Stella has a lot of anger from somewhere—that's

for sure. I think she's rolled all the past and present angers up into one giant anger and that that part of her brain is full, like the memory of a computer.

She must have had a bad day working at the convenience store. I stood in the living room and watched her through the open bedroom door as she pulled shirt after shirt out of the closet. She tossed them on the floor with one hand while she tried to pull up and fasten her jeans with the other. "Where's my black shirt?" she yelled.

I winced. "It's probably in the dryer."

"Couldn't you have put the clothes away so they wouldn't wrinkle? Hell, I worked my butt off all day. The least you can do is help out, Judith." When I heard Stella walk into the bathroom, I tiptoed across the kitchen to the dryer. It was such a luxury! A washer and dryer in our own place.

"I couldn't get to it. I got a call last night to babysit the kid next door. The noisy five-year-old." I found the shirt in the dryer.

"Oh," Stella said.

"Here's your shirt. I've got it. I'll iron it," I said.

"Thanks." She was putting on makeup, and she yelled out, "I met a man last night. A trucker. I'm praying to anything that listens—Buddha, Jesus Christ, or Allah—to bring him back to the bar tonight. I got a good feeling about him."

"I guess you'll bring him over before too long," I said.

"Yeah, if I'm lucky," she answered. She walked into the living room in her black bra and jeans. She's thin. It's probably from all the nervous energy she expends. She was brushing her long blond-streaked hair. "It's hotter than hell in here." She walked over to the miniblinds and yanked the cord. It broke and they crashed to the floor.

"Shit!" She came over to the ironing board, grabbed the half-ironed shirt from me, pulled it on, and walked out the door, buttoning on her way. "That's it! I'm out of here."

I found a pink-and-white-striped sheet in an unpacked box and hung it over the window.

Two

Two weeks into school, John Mark Miller stood up in honors poetry class to read his poem. I'd studied him and Jasmine Hess since the first day. Sometimes they ate lunch together. They seemed closer than friends, but they didn't do the usual girlfriend-boyfriend stuff. No arms around each other or pinches on the butt.

Maybe moving so much had turned me into an observer. I always watched people, especially interesting ones. John Mark and Jasmine fit that definition. I couldn't describe them using the normal categories, except that he was a senior, a millennial grad like me, and she was a junior. In this little town everything and everyone is so defined, and John Mark and Jasmine didn't fit the groups: prep or straight, freak or goth, townie or thug, hick or jock. Either they were floaters or just utterly oblivious.

John Mark had broad, flat cheekbones, a square jaw, kind of thin lips, and long blond hair that he usually wore in a ponytail. He wasn't skinny, just lean. He was average height, but he seemed taller because his long arms were usually waving around expressing something.

When he recited his poem, he made his voice flat, doing the depressed robot routine. He had it perfect, straight from *Hitchhiker's Guide to the Galaxy*.

When I was ten, Stella "checked out" the entire taped book, and we listened to it while we were moving to Birmingham, Alabama, a move inspired by the song "Sweet Home Alabama" by Lynyrd Skynyrd. Stella heard the song while driving home after a particularly nasty fight with Eric, I think it was. The names of her boyfriends all run together. It was one in the morning, and by one the next afternoon, we were on our way to Alabama. Stella had done the robot routine while she was driving, but she'd never gotten the voice down.

I broke my own silence rule and laughed out loud in class. Then I couldn't stop laughing. John Mark was too good! His brown eyes were as flat as his drone voice. He could probably imitate anything, plant, human, or animal. Maybe imitation was the key to being a floater. I decided he was a floater.

Jasmine, who was in my poetry class and my art class, was a floater too. She was small, but I didn't think of her that way because she had so much energy. Her nearly black eyes were big, and her short spiky hair was dark. Her smile seemed wide, but I think that's just because her teeth were so little and white and her lips were a dark plum color, naturally, not artificially.

She played drums in the school jazz band, and she ran cross-country on the boys' team because she was that good. She didn't seem to care what people thought, or at least that's what her clothes said. They weren't "I'm edgy," or "I'm into all black—anger and death," or "I'm expensive and cool." Her style was definitely her own. Indefinable.

John Mark and Jasmine had said stuff to me, even though I didn't answer back. I did my usual half smile, glance down, and cover my face with my hair trick. It looked shy and usually put most people off.

When I was little, I'd tried my best to get some school friends, and I even had some, but it hurt too much when we moved and I had to leave them behind. All that wondering what had happened to Elise and Sharon, and all that wondering if they ever thought of me. All that starting over again.

In high school, new kids were the object of curiosity or pity. I didn't need or want either. By then

I'd also realized that my life wasn't exactly like most other kids', not "normal," and I really didn't want to open my roving life to their inspection.

As John Mark and I walked out of the room after the robot routine, he said, "So . . . are you going to get small now?"

My usual tricks hadn't put him off, so I decided to see where things would go. Maybe it was a now-or-never moment, so I said, "What?"

"You know what I mean," he replied, and then he spelled, "S-M-A-L-L. You seem to know all about it." He switched to the depressed robot voice and went on: "The survival skills of small." I smiled in spite of myself.

Jasmine caught up with us and said, "Rule number one: Don't look people in the eyes. Rule number two: Always walk at the edge of the hallway. Rule number three: Never speak to someone else first." She turned and looked at me. *Uh-oh,* I thought, and then in a flash I had it.

So I said, "Rule number four: Don't volunteer answers in class. Rule number five: If the teacher asks you a question, say as little as possible."

"And last but not least," John Mark said, "rule number six: Don't let anyone know how smart you really are."

By that time, we were at a hall junction to the

lunchroom. "I thought you'd be good at small," John Mark said. "I haven't seen you talk to anyone since you've been here, but I could tell you weren't shy."

"This is cool," Jasmine said. "You know, like we've been here before. Like it's supposed to be. Déjà vu and all that. Sit with us?"

"Sure," I said. Why not? They were fun. I sat down at the gray plastic tables with John Mark and Jasmine. They talked about the tryouts for the school play while I sketched. It was *Romeo and Juliet,* and John Mark was trying for Romeo. Jasmine said that no one else even had a chance.

At the end of lunch, Jasmine stood up and said, "See you tomorrow," and then as she turned to go, she said, "And you can call me Jazz. With two *z*'s. All my friends do."

Todd Rineer was walking into the cafeteria as we were walking out. He was heading toward a table full of jocks. I'd noticed him on the first day of school. He was in my art class and left a little early to get to football practice. I overheard him say it to Ms. Dennis, and it had intrigued me. An artist who plays football isn't your usual combination; besides, he was good to look at.

He had curly dark hair and tanned skin. His nose was a little flat, but he was in sports, so it had probably gotten smashed at some point. He was big, but solid, like he was holding a lot of muscle in check.

After school I shuffled along the edge of the road and thought about John Mark and Jazz. Friends? Me? What a novel concept. I'd just take things a little at a time, slow like, and see where they went. To my way of thinking, trust was earned and I'd seen little reason for it in the past.

I stuck my hands deep in the pockets of my green fatigues, my favorite pants, and thought about small. What a great name for it! I'd been learning small all my life. As we moved from city to city, the schools got bigger and tougher, so small got easier.

Like John Mark had said, it was a matter of survival. Small took on the pain; it took the swirling thoughts away for a tiny space. It dropped them in a pocket, like a used tissue, but also like a used tissue, they could be found again, all crumpled, at the most unlikely moment.

Ms. Dennis had told us on the first day of school that there was a special exhibit of van Gogh's portraits at the Philadelphia Art Museum and that we were going to see it. I couldn't believe it! A field trip to get excited about. Because the art class was so small, we went in two of the vans that were usually used by athletic teams. Jazz was late, but just as we were about to pull out of the parking lot, she banged on Ms. Dennis's window, then ran around and climbed in the van.

She squeezed in the seat ahead of me, and we smiled at each other. The van creaked, and air squealed through the bad window seals. People were buzzing all around me. Jazz put headphones on, and soon her head was bobbing. I wondered what she was listening to, and then I turned to stare out the window at the trees. The green sameness put me to sleep. Eventually I woke up because someone was poking me. I looked over to see Jazz leaning way back over the seat.

"We're almost there. Look at the sculptures," she said.

I stared out at the stone figures by the river. "Cool." Their bodies were massive and so many of their faces were sad. I couldn't imagine making them.

We parked and got out. The museum was packed. People everywhere. It was difficult to move without bumping into someone. At the desk they gave us brochures with maps of the exhibits. The place was huge. I put my finger on the YOU ARE HERE. I knew where I was, where I wanted to go, and that I could actually get there on my own.

Slowly because of the crush of people, I found my way to the van Gogh exhibit. Jazz was close behind me.

I put on the headset and turned on the tour of the exhibit. The audio told the story of all the paintings. Jazz didn't use the audio set. She looked like she was going to stay in the part of the display that showed van Gogh's early drawings. They were black-and-white sketches of poor people with mournful expressions.

I moved through the whole exhibit, but I was drawn back to the self-portraits. In one he had a felt hat, and in another he had a straw hat. I saw his artistic vision crying to be released when I looked into his hollow eyes. I could see the frenetic, dispossessed cells of his mind bumping against each other. I was writing my paper about him. No doubt. I wanted to know what his dreams and struggles were. Were they like mine? I saw that Jazz was standing beside me.

"What are you looking at?" she asked.

"The eyes."

"Yeah," Jazz said. "Deep, sort of piercing-like."

Because I'd been into the eyes, I spoke without thinking: "I look through those eyes every day."

"God, you mean that?" Jazz said. Without waiting for me to answer, she went on: "That would be intense." Then she was quiet, and I felt squirmy. Like a dried-out worm on the pavement trying to make it back to the wet grass. A jiggly laugh came out of the corner of my mouth.

"Tiring anyway," I said, trying to use a safer word to cover what I'd said. I'd just crossed into the trust realm without giving it enough thought. I hadn't known her that long.

Jazz barked out a little laugh, so maybe she was uncomfortable too. She said, "Come on. Let's go see his sunflower painting."

I leaned my head toward the straw-hat portrait and tipped an imaginary hat. "So long, Vincent. I'll be seeing you," I whispered. Jazz grabbed my arm and pulled me. It seemed I hadn't freaked her out too much.

We threaded slowly in and out of the crowd until we were standing in front of the sunflower painting. "I love this," Jazz said. "I mean, why the one brown sunflower down in the corner?"

"Composition," I said. "You need it. You need the"—I paused, searching for the right word— "unexpected."

"You're right," Ms. Dennis said. I jumped. She was standing right beside me. Gooseflesh rose on my arms; I hadn't heard her walk up. "I never thought of it that way before, but it definitely invites a question, and art should leave space for that."

I kept my eyes glued on the picture. That was cool. From the first day of school, Ms. Dennis had stood out to me. Not just another blah-blah talking face. Someone who possibly got things that other adults didn't quite see.

She was one of the last authentic hippies. A living, breathing memorial to the sixties. Ms. Dennis walked in a quiet, rolling motion in her Birkenstock sandals. She wore floor-length gauzy dresses from India that swayed around her, or peasant blouses and skirts that looked like they came from Central America. She had long, frizzy gray hair. Although I couldn't prove it, I guessed she did yoga every night and ate soy dogs at least once a week.

Even though I liked Ms. Dennis, I was a little afraid of her. She was the sort of person who made you want to try things without asking you. A rare thing in a teacher.

"It's twelve thirty. Have you had your lunches?" she asked us.

"No," Jazz and I said at the same time. We walked back with her to the vans and got our lunches. I also grabbed my sketchbook. Jazz and I walked along the river, stopping to read the inscriptions about the sculptures. They were sculptures of the different immigrants who had come to America. Some people were out rowing on the river. I picked a wall to sit on to eat my lunch, and Jazz scrambled up onto one of the sculptures to eat hers. I finished eating and started sketching one of van Gogh's self-portraits.

I looked up from a sketch and saw that Todd Rineer was walking toward me. He was looking down, and when he looked up, I smiled at him. He smiled back, and I saw red blush streaks sneaking out of the collar of his T-shirt and up his neck. He sat on a bench by himself.

"You rated a smile. Impressive," Jazz said.

"Why do you say that?" I asked.

Jazz said, "He's seen me plenty of times before, and I didn't get a smile like that."

"Maybe it was because I smiled first," I said.

"Clever thought," Jazz replied. "It probably didn't hurt that you're pretty and new in town. Maybe he even thinks you're"—Jazz paused and raised her eyebrows—"mysterious."

"Yeah, right," I said. "What's his story?" I didn't have any classes with Todd besides art, and I was curious. I'd never known a football player who'd even remotely interested me before.

"He's smart, like really intelligent. Takes a bunch of science and math classes I wouldn't be caught dead in. Not to imply, of course, that I *could* be in them. Why he's in art class, I don't know," Jazz said. "It's not like I know him well. His parents have a dairy farm, and I think he works a lot. During football season he shines, but I think he's kind of quiet."

I watched Todd while she talked. He was watching the rowers as he ate. I hadn't seen him with a girl, but I was waiting to see if Jazz was going to say something about someone. When she didn't, I said, "Maybe he's shy."

He stopped eating and stood up. I watched him walking away and thought of the art class. He was better than most of the people in there. People probably focused on his football and intelligence, the "what you're good at" stuff. Maybe there was a lot about him people didn't know.

"Could be. I've never hung around the jocks or the farmers, and he's usually with one of those groups," Jazz said.

Few people look beyond the surface, I thought. My life was evidence of that. It's so rare to find someone who sees past the obvious. I wondered where I was going with those thoughts. I jumped off the wall. I'd sworn off boys a while ago, and it would take something incredibly momentous to change that decision.

"Hello," Jazz said. "Did you hear what I said?"

"Something about . . ." I paused and then laughed. "Nope," I answered.

Three

That Saturday, Stella was working second shift, which meant that life was quieter. I lay in bed reading for a while. Spider-Man slept and woke up and lay there thumping his tail. We were good together as usual. Spider-Man could kill spiders, which I couldn't, climb walls, which I couldn't, and keep secrets, which was something I absolutely counted on. Friends like Spider-Man are rare.

I got on the city bus and headed for the library to look for a book on van Gogh. I was looking forward to finding out more about him. As we drove out of E-ville, we passed a few dairy farms. Most of the black-and-white cows ignored the sound of the bus and kept their heads down, chewing away, but one did look up, then right back down.

I didn't get it. Are bovines naturally arrogant, or is grass that interesting?

We went through two more small towns on our way into the city. In between the towns, the corn was tall. There were a lot of people outside because the weather was nice. While we were at a bus stop, I looked across the street and saw a woman on a front porch swing. She waved at me, and I waved back. The woman had little white bows all around the collar of her blue T-shirt. There were matching bows on the sleeves and white bows on the knees of her capri pants. She even had white sandals with little bows. What was with the bows?

This lady was bow-deprived. I decided that the woman's mother had died when she was three, but before her final day on God's earth, she had hugged her little girl to her chest. The white bow on the mother's robe made an imprint on the girl's cheek. And this bow memory still comforted her.

I had watched a lot of soaps, but I got so good at figuring out what people were going to say and do even before they did that it got boring. I could have written the plots. I'd taken to figuring out real people instead. Far more interesting.

At the library, I found a biography called *Vincent*

van Gogh: A Life. As I stood in line at the checkout counter, the broad-shouldered back of the person two people ahead of me got my attention. And what a fine black-leathered back it was. It was Todd, and this was as close as I'd ever gotten to him. I stepped aside as the woman in front of me hefted a large bag of books up on the counter. Todd was turning to leave at the same time, and we nearly collided.

"Oh," I said. "Sorry."

At the same time Todd said, "Excuse me."

Why had I said anything? Why didn't I wait for him to say something first? We both laughed the awkward laugh, the kind that makes you wish you had stifled it. How embarrassing!

"Can I help you?" the librarian asked.

"Oh yeah. Here," I said, turning back to face her. I handed her my book and card. When she handed them back to me and I turned away from the counter, Todd was still standing there, waiting for me. Shock stopped my feet, but thank God, some instinct kicked in and moved them. He walked with me to the door and glanced down at the book I was carrying.

"For art class?" he asked.

"Yeah," I said. I wanted to think of something clever, but my clever brain had checked out at the counter.

"Me too." He held up a book with one of Monet's water-lily pictures on the cover.

"Do you like Monet?" I said.

"Yeah. My parents have this picture over their bed. They also have a big book sitting on the coffee table, full of Impressionist paintings."

"Oh," I said. "So, you know a lot about the Impressionists?"

"Not really. I used to look at the paintings in the book, and the title, *The Impressionists,* was on the cover." He grinned. "Since I liked the paintings, I figured it was time to learn more."

I laughed and said, "At least you're honest. Van Gogh for me."

"I hadn't seen much of his stuff before the field trip," Todd said.

"I've loved his work for a long time." I stared at the van Gogh book as if it was the only thing that existed on the planet. I decided to risk a glance at Todd's face, and he was looking at me. We both looked away.

In the parking lot, he stopped by a midnight-blue truck. It had little silver specks that glinted in the sun. "Here's my truck," he said with a lift of pride in his voice.

"I like the color," I said.

"Where's your car?" he asked, looking around.

"I don't have one," I answered.

"Hey, let me give you a ride."

"Sure," I said. A trip with him and no long bus ride to the apartment! Sounded good to me. I climbed into the truck.

"I've got to get home to help my dad," Todd said.

"What does he do?" I asked, like I didn't already know.

"He's a farmer, and harvest is the busiest season. We milk too."

I couldn't think of anything to say to that. Todd said some more stuff about farming. I listened, but I was more aware of his arm on the steering wheel and his leg on the seat only six inches from me. It was instant electricity.

"You can drop me off in the square," I said when we got close to E-ville. I didn't want him seeing where I lived. Not yet.

"See you in art," Todd said.

I nodded. "Thanks for the ride." The words "See you in art" went round and round in my mind. As I walked home, I made those words last. It was like licking a raspberry soft-serve ice-cream cone on Labor Day when the Freeze and Frosty was closing for the season.

Inside the apartment I went straight to my room, plopped on the lump of a mattress that I called a bed, and thought about Todd. Was it good luck or what? Imagine meeting him in the library over books on artists.

I couldn't help going over every word that had been said. Of course I mostly thought about what I *should* have said. When I'd had enough—you can only beat yourself up so long—I began reading the biography. The author, Philip Callow, wrote:

> All at once tragedy struck. Eleven months after their marriage, a son, Vincent Willem, was born. The infant was stillborn. Anna was thirty-three, about to have her deepest wish fulfilled. The crib, carefully and lovingly prepared, stood in a corner and mocked them. A pale silent Christ on a cross looked down, in a church cold and clammy like a tomb. The dead child was buried in the church graveyard.

The book went on to say that exactly a year later, van Gogh's parents had another boy and they also named him Vincent Willem. I felt a prickle in my neck. I stopped reading and put the book down beside me. I looked up at the glow-in-the-dark stars that were stuck on my ceiling. The prickle radiated out into goose bumps that shivered down my arms. *My God,* I thought. *Named after a dead baby, just like me.*

Had Vincent's mother gotten over the loss of her first baby? My mother hadn't. That conversation had its own wrinkle in my brain. It was the most memorable of my life.

On my fourteenth birthday, which was three and a half years ago, I went to a party thrown by some older kids down the street and lost my virginity. *Lost* is a good term for what happened because it was gone, and it wasn't like I got something great in return for it. I figured a fourteenth birthday was a good time to have sex. Kids I knew at school were having it, and I didn't want to wait too long, so I went to the party and got drunk with some guy. The next thing I remembered was smiling stupidly at his blurred face above mine, and pain below, between my legs. I rolled over when it was done and fell off the bed. And that's all I remember. Don't even know who the guy was.

About two in the morning, I stumbled toward home, aware of the pain. I had this idea that I would talk to Stella about sex. By that time in my life, we weren't on the best of terms, but I figured she'd talk to me about sex because she referred to it all the time. There had to be something good about it. Something I'd missed. I really needed to talk to someone, and moms were supposed to be good for stuff like that. I was too drunk to think through this expectation, but it was there.

When I opened the door, my mother said, "Where in the hell have you been? I've been waiting up all night for you."

Not true, I thought. *You've been waiting for someone, but it sure wasn't me.* I didn't say a word, though. I'd learned long before that it was better not to interrupt Stella's flow. Out and over was a good damage control strategy where my mother was concerned. Her drunk tongue was dangerous.

"I almost called the cops," she went on.

I doubt it, I thought. If my mother called the cops, they would find her drunk and unable to take care of herself, much less me.

Stella had fibbed—her word—for so long that she rattled her lies off without thinking. It was like she actually believed them as they tumbled out of her mouth.

I'd taken my usual stance, legs apart, stiff and braced, with my arms crossed over my stomach. If a big lie was coming, it would be yelled. Stella seemed to think that volume made her lies real.

But she didn't yell that time. Instead, she paused.

"I wish I'd kept the first baby, Judith Lee." Each word was slow, and not very loud. Each word was being thought about before being spoken. "Dammit," she said a little louder, "I wish I kept the first baby." There was no slur in her words.

I sobered up in one dead second. "She would have been a perfect little girl. I had the name Judith Lee picked out for her. I would have kept that baby except that her dad left me for no good reason. Without a word, damn him. I mean I saw red. I really loved that stinking man, and he left me high and dry. What else could I do?

"I thought your dad was gonna be better, but he was worse. Tried to kick you to death when I was pregnant, so I decided right there on the floor to keep you just to spite him. And then I gave you her name. The one I picked out for the first baby." Then Stella stood up, smoothed down her shirt, and walked out of the room.

The sour came up to the hollow above my lungs. It was looking to fill the back of my throat. I sat down, put my head between my knees, and kept swallowing, swallowing, staring at my feet. What sort of woman lived at the end of a man's foot? Did his shoes make her decisions? I puked on my own shoes. I slipped out of them and ran to the bathroom.

I rinsed my mouth and spat, and rinsed and spat again. I took a scalding hot shower. "I was born just for spite," I said to the showerhead. I hated the dead cells on my skin; I scrubbed everywhere until I felt raw. I wanted to scrub away the spite and sex. The drunken sex was too much like Stella.

"Call me Spitebaby," I said to Spider-Man, who was lying on the bed beside me. Then I yelled, "Spitebaby, Spitebaby, Spitebaby!" Spider-Man burrowed under the covers, just like he did when Stella started yelling.

"Sorry, Spider-Man, I didn't mean to scare you. You and me, we is best friends." That didn't bring him out. "Come on out," I said. When Spider-Man still didn't come out, I pulled back the covers and stroked his back.

I vowed on that birthday that I would never, ever, be like my mother. I disowned her. I never got drunk again, and I stopped chasing boys. I wanted the vow to be solemn and binding. It had to be a blood vow, but since there wasn't anyone but me to vow with, I took some scissors and drew a line of blood on each of my own wrists and I rubbed them together.

And I changed my name from Judith to Jude. Not Judith Lee. Plain old Jude, like the Beatles song.

The thumping of Spider-Man's tail brought me back from age fourteen. I was all curled up. I stretched out. Had my father's shoes left permanent bruises inside of me, in my brain? Stella left him right after I was born. I had no memory of him.

I don't remember any other guy kicking or hitting her. I do remember a man—well, I remember a muscular arm thick with black hair—punching a wall. It's one of my first memories; I must have been about three. He put a bunny-shaped hole in the wall. A huddled bunny with little ears. Maybe he was the guy after my dad. But after that guy, Stella didn't stick around any man for too long if fists started flying. One thing I knew for sure: I didn't want to be anything like her. One man to the next, one baby to the next.

I saw the van Gogh book lying next to me where I'd left it when my thoughts had gone back to that conversation. I flipped it over and traced the sketch of Vincent's tortured-eyed face with my finger. What else did Vincent and I have in common? Did his mind ache? I wanted the swirling thoughts to stop, so I could sleep a lot. Eight hours even. The insomniac's dream.

I concentrated on the *thump, thump, thump* of Spider-Man's tail, willing the rhythm to take me to sleep.

Four

I couldn't believe my luck. In art class the next week, Todd and I were put at the same table for pottery! Had to be a miracle. I kept sneaking peaks at him. My head only came to his shoulder. I wished I could see his eyes, but he was next to me at the table. As we worked with the clay, I watched his hands. I'd never noticed a man's hands before. Hands were important, I decided as I watched his forming the narrow neck of his vase. It was much better than mine.

Ms. Dennis called his name. He turned around to look at her, and as he did, he hit my vase with his left hand. It rolled across the table, but then he caught it with his right hand before it hit the floor. What reflexes! His ears were red, and his neck was blotchy with pinkish marks when he handed it back to me. He didn't look at me when he said, "Sorry."

"It's okay. It wasn't hurt," I replied.

People at the other tables were chatting away as we worked, but there was a soft quiet at our table. It surrounded us. Home base in a game of tag.

Todd glanced up at the clock, and then said, "I've got to get going. Football. You want to go to a movie Saturday night?"

Was he talking to me? I looked over at him, and his brown eyes were definitely looking at me, so I figured he was. I sucked in air so hard that I lost my voice for a moment. "Yeah, sure," I answered.

As he stood up, he said, "Quick, write your number down." I scribbled my phone number on a sheet of paper and then ripped it out of my notebook and handed it to him.

As I walked home, the air itself was bright, touchable. I held up my hands and let it flow through my fingers. Then I watched as the light glanced on a maple that had the faintest touch of orange, and reflected off it in perfect rays. A woman in an old green housedress was setting out pots of mauve and gold mums on her porch. I waved at her and she waved back. Even the window in K & L's Pizza seemed cleaner.

The glass caught the pale lightness of my skin. When I was little, I thought my skin was see-through, because you could see the blue in lots of my veins, and I thought the light sprinkling of freckles were buttons that kept my skin fastened in place.

The light that day made my eyes look dark. I wondered if Todd noticed the slight tilt of my eyes. The tilt didn't go with the fact that they were deep-set with lots of dark eyelashes. Not my mom's eyes. And my small but not snub nose was definitely not hers. Both of these features make me wonder what my dad looked like, but that's all I wonder about him. I don't want to know anything else.

Blue-and-white streamers flew from some of the trees in the square. A yellow-and-orange neon sign blinked in the hobby train store. The trim on the furniture-refinishing store was freshly painted in purple and green. Every detail was pure color and contrast.

As I walked up the hill toward the railroad tracks, I slung my backpack to my other shoulder; it was too heavy with the extra van Gogh book in it. I couldn't wait to read some more.

That day's chapters were about first love. His was intense and tragic. No other words for it. He loved Eugenia, but she didn't love him back. Vincent wouldn't give up on her, even though she was engaged to someone else and wouldn't have anything to do with him. The pain lived inside of him as a permanent sorrow, a parasite that ate away at him.

That chapter of van Gogh's biography reminded me of Stella's story. Maybe she'd never gotten over her first love, and that's why she never settled into another man. What would have happened if that first man had been different?

I'd had lots of "boyfriends," but nothing real. They were all just stupid junior-high flirts, and after Stella's story on my birthday, I'd made myself scarce. Besides, we didn't stick around anywhere long enough.

I knew that my first real love would be as intense as van Gogh's, no getting around it, but unlike van Gogh and my mother, I would choose well, and that would make all the difference. There wouldn't be any permanent sorrow, no parasites eating me all my life.

I pictured Todd Rineer. He was good at sports, art, and school, and he came from a real family. The kind that went to your games, knew your teacher's name, and sat around the table eating dinner together. He seemed just the type to rescue me from my present life. I closed the book and stood up.

The next day after school, I went to see Gram. As I was taking care of the African violets, I said, "There's this guy at school I've been watching since the beginning of the year. God, that makes me sound like a stalker or something. What I really mean is that I've just been observing or noticing him—but not chasing him. I asked Jazz about him, and she said he was smart and his dad's a farmer. He doesn't have a girlfriend."

Sounds good. Tell me more.

"He's in my art class, and I ran into him at the library—the city library, not the school one. We were both looking for books about artists for our project, the one I told you about, and we talked about artists. He gave me a ride home."

Feels like destiny to me.

"Definitely. I mean it was like fate or karma or something. And then yesterday in art we were put at the same table. And he knocked my vase and caught it. He blushed—I think he's kind of shy."

Nothing sounds bad so far.

"I know. He sounds too good to be true, doesn't he? Knowing my life, he probably is. I think he comes from this normal farm family. And what I'm trying to say"—I took a deep breath—"is that he's asked me out. Can you believe it? I mean he's a football player, he takes all the advanced math classes, and I'm new and . . ." My voice trailed off. I realized that I hadn't done any cleaning or tidying yet in Gram's room. I began cleaning the sink.

It sounds like you're a little afraid, which I can

understand. There are always risks, but he sounds good, and besides, you're just getting to know him. How can it hurt? But it almost sounds like you are trying to convince me of something.

"Well"—I pulled a chair over close to her bed—"it's just that I swore off boys. I don't want to be like Stella, constantly chasing men, picking the wrong ones, and moving to find the next."

You don't need to worry about that. You are nothing like your mother. I'm sure you will make good choices. I trust you.

"Thanks, Gram," I said. I kissed her and got up. "I love you," I said.

I love you too.

When I got home after seeing Gram, I saw a note from my mother on the kitchen table. She said that Irma, our neighbor, whom I hadn't met yet, had called. I called Irma back, and she wanted me to babysit. I said I'd love to, hoping it would be a regular thing. I needed the money. I hadn't babysat the five-year-old next door after that first time. Irma said to come on over.

I knocked on her door. A newspaper was lying by my foot, so I bent down to pick it up. The door opened, and I was staring at tiny feet in pink velveteen ballet slippers—had to be a size five. As I stood up, I saw thick rubbery legs in pink leggings and a big body in a fuschia tunic-top. How did those feet hold up that body? They didn't seem to go together. Another of life's mysteries.

"Hi, I'm Irma. My baby Tommy's already asleep, so you won't have to do much. I'll be back at eleven."

"Okay," I said. Irma was right. I didn't do anything with Tommy. I read more than half of the biography while I was there.

As I read about van Gogh's life, a desolation thing settled on me. It wasn't mind ache; maybe it was a subtle shading of sadness. It was a blue, deep midnight blue. I'd successfully pushed the pain away for a while, but I knew it hadn't really left. It had just been sitting at the edge of my mind like the crow at the railroad tracks, always watching, always wanting to remind me that it couldn't be gotten rid of that easily. It had its turf.

For my date with Todd that Saturday, I wore my best jeans, which wasn't a hard decision because I only had two pairs, and I wore my purple good-luck sweater. The movie was *The Mummy*. I tried to watch, but . . . what can I say? Adventure movies have to be excellent, and this one wasn't. I tried not to look bored.

"There were some good parts, weren't there?"

Todd said afterward. His voice went up on the words *weren't there*.

I laughed. The only good part of the movie that I could think of was that Brendan Fraser, the star, looked a lot like Todd. The other thing was that Todd's arm was around me. "The sand in the movie was nice," I said. "I like walking in sand, but I think I'd prefer the beach to the desert."

"Me too," he said. As he pushed both his hands into his jean pockets, I could just see his brain clicking, asking himself if that was a dumb thing to say. "What I mean is I like to walk on the beach too. My family goes to the shore every summer."

"Cool," I said. I couldn't imagine going to the shore with your family every summer. "We lived in California when I was little. My mom and I used to go to the beach."

"That's sweet. I've lived here all my life. Same house even. I wish I'd lived somewhere else, maybe even for a summer just to see what it is like. Have you lived in other places?"

"Yes. We've moved a lot." I wasn't about to go into any more of that. Not yet. I wanted to get the conversation back to him, but my breath was a little tight in my upper chest and throat. I was afraid my voice would come out strange, like high or something, so I gulped hard without looking too obvious, I hoped. When I said, "I think living in one house all your life would be great," my voice came out okay.

"You want to go somewhere and talk?"

"Yeah," I said. This was the part I was looking forward to—finding out more about him. Walking on the beach had sounded good. I could see Todd and me walking in the sand right at the water's edge. I brought myself back from the daydream; he was talking.

"You want to go to Pizza City?"

"Yes." As we drove, I could hear Stella's slightly boozy voice in my mind. This was from a one-way late-night conversation right before my fourteenth birthday. I'd been trying to watch *Saturday Night Live*. "Men are interested in themselves—it's a fact. So I get them to talk about themselves. I never yammer away about me. Men don't like that." Then she added, "And I never ask them about feelings. Uh-uh. Don't go there. They don't like that, and besides, you might not want to know. Take it from me." If sheer number was the determining factor, Stella was an expert at getting men to talk; she was lousy at keeping them, though. Must be you had to know something different for that.

I got my brain in gear. I asked, "So what do you like to do?"

"I like playing football obviously, and hunting. Deer hunting. I'd like to go out west and hunt elk, but

I haven't had a chance yet. I like hiking too. Just being outdoors, I guess."

"I like hiking," I said. I thought you could qualify walks along the railroad tracks as hiking. I liked the outdoors, but I hated any thought of hunting.

"Sorry, but I'm not into hunting." I felt like I had to say that. When Todd started smiling, I said, "Don't get me wrong, I'm not a Bambi lover or anything. It's just that whenever I see a head mounted on a wall, I have to look away. I can feel the deer's eyes following me, hunting me wherever I go in the room. Who can blame the deer for haunting people?"

"Haunting? I haven't really looked at a stuffed deer's eyes, but . . . but I haven't heard of many girls who are into hunting. I'm glad you like hiking. We'll go sometime."

This sounded good to me. Sounded like he was thinking about the future. We got out of his truck and headed into Pizza City. It was crowded and hot. We had to wait a while for a table, so Todd ordered a pizza. One guy came over and slapped him on the shoulder saying, "Good game last night. Keep it up. Banefield Central next week."

Another guy walked up and high-fived him and said, "What did you think of that quarterback?"

I felt myself getting small. School wasn't the only place it happened. It happened a lot, especially in places with too many people and too little space, like busy streets, or malls at Christmas. I got opaque. It was amazing, but when I didn't transmit light, people didn't see me. I could still see them, hear them, feel them bouncing off of my surface.

"Either his passing was off last night or he isn't nearly as good as he's talked up," Todd said. "See you around." He turned back to me as Jazz whizzed by in her Pizza City uniform, bumping me with her shoulder.

"Follow me, Jude," she said. "I'll get you a table." I followed her. "There," she said, pointing to a table in the corner. As we sat down, she leaned over and whispered, "I was right about the smile."

"Shut up," I said. Jazz just grinned. Todd sat down, and I sat down across from him, planting my feet on the floor and folding my arms on the table. Grounding myself.

"What do you want to do after high school?" he asked me when the pizza came.

"I really haven't thought a lot about it," I answered.

"I'm hoping for a football scholarship to a Big Ten school. I'm going to college to get a degree in agribusiness. My older brother is going to farm with my dad."

"What's agribusiness?" I asked. I didn't want to

sound dumb, but I didn't know. I pulled the crust off my piece of pizza and took my first bite.

"The business part of farming. Buying and selling grains, fertilizer, and equipment. Shipping stuff." Todd picked up his second piece of pizza.

I couldn't think of anything to say to that, so I moved on to something I'd wanted to know more about. "What about art? Do you like it?"

"Yes, but I don't know much about it. I guess there hasn't been much time for it, with football, working on the farm, and math classes for college. I'm glad I'm in that class, though. I'm learning a lot." Todd went on to eat his third piece of pizza, while I finished my first.

Jazz came flying by and Todd said, "I'm really thirsty. One can isn't going to do it. Just bring a pitcher." He smiled and, without a drop of embarrassment, wiped away a piece of cheese that had fallen on his chin. He downed a glass of Coke in record time after Jazz brought the pitcher. I watched his hand, which reminded me of pottery.

"You are really good at pottery," I said without thinking. Todd pulled the tab back and forth on his empty Coke can until it came off. I could tell he was a little embarrassed by my words.

"You really think so?" he said. He ate another piece of pizza.

"Yeah," I said. "And I've looked at lots of art." I poured some catsup, dipped the crust of my pizza into it, and started eating it. I liked his question. What I thought really mattered, and he believed I knew more about something than he did. That was a good sign.

"Enough of me. What about you? You must like art." He wanted to know about me. Another good sign.

"I love seeing and doing art, especially drawing and painting. I've loved them since I was little. When I draw, I create another world." It came out in a rush. I'd almost forgotten to breathe, so I slowed down, looked down at my hands, and said, "Other worlds make life in this world more possible. Believable." I'd taken a pen out of my purse when I finished eating, my usual habit when I was out somewhere. I drew stars that became eyes on the napkin. "I'm thinking about being an artist someday." Todd was quiet, so I stopped drawing. I looked up, but he wasn't looking at my hand. He was looking at my face.

Todd said, "I've never heard anyone say something like that. Creating another world . . . that's cool." He stood up. "We better get going. I'm beat and milking's at four."

Both of us were quiet on the way home. I leaned my head against the seat, easing the muscles in my neck. I hadn't realized that I was tense, but as the relief flooded through me, everything relaxed. He wasn't some sort of jerk. I liked what I had heard about Todd, and he seemed to like me.

When Todd pulled up in front of the apartment, he turned and said, "Can I see you again?"

"Yes. And thanks for the movie." Todd leaned over and kissed me on the cheek. I turned to look at him, and he kissed my mouth. It was soft. "See you on Monday."

As I walked up the stairs, I touched my lips and thought, *Yes, yes, yes.* This wasn't bad. Maybe this guy was different. Maybe he was the one.

I pulled off my jeans and got into bed. Was it really possible? Could my life change? I heard Stella trying to get her key in the door. When she finally got the lock open, she stumbled over the threshold.

The ache that crowded my mind on bad days was only lingering on the edges that night. This thing with Todd, whatever it was, seemed good. Was it too good? I told myself to stop thinking about him for fear it would jinx things. I stroked Spider-Man, hoping to fall asleep, but it was hard to not think about Todd, and that kept me awake.

Five

"Look what I found," John Mark said at the lunch table that Tuesday. Jazz walked up and sat down beside him. We'd been having lunch together since the small day, three weeks earlier. Having people to sit with during lunch had greatly improved what had always been one of the worst parts of my school day.

I liked Jazz and John Mark, and felt okay around them. Our lunchroom talks tended to have that "intellectual" air that I'd heard when listening in on other "smart" kid conversations, and that was fine by me. It felt good to flex my brain, and besides, I didn't want to say that much anyway. I mostly let Jazz and John Mark do the talking, and they liked to watch me draw.

I was drawing in my sketchbook, and one of the cafeteria cooks took shape under my hand, with dots for eyes, a scooped nose, and billowing hair. I always drew during lunch. Gray plastic everywhere dulled my appetite.

John Mark put a paperback book on the table. It was called *Dear Theo,* and it had one of van Gogh's self-portraits on the cover. I stared at it and looked up at John Mark. "Jazz has talked on and on about the van Gogh exhibit, so when I saw this at the Goodwill store, I bought it. Along with this shirt." He pointed to his yellow T-shirt with the word *Cheerios* across it. "They were each fifty cents."

"Hey, I got this shirt at Goodwill last week too," Jazz said. She was wearing a black lace shirt over a silver tank top. Her pierced eyebrow had a new ring with a black stone that reflected the light. She pulled at the lace collar and widened her large eyes. When she did this, you could see white above her irises. "Mad cool, huh!"

"Anyway," John Mark said, pausing to emphasize that he'd been interrupted, "it's a book of van Gogh's letters to his brother. Listen to this." He opened the book and read, "'There is safety in the midst of danger. What would life be if we had no courage to attempt anything?' I love it."

"Interesting," I said. It sounded like walking on the railroad tracks. "I agree with that."

"The end of the quote sounds like you, Jazz," John Mark went on. "Because he talks about fighting, winning, and going for the best."

"Yep," Jazz said. "Pure Jazz."

I'd never met anyone who had the courage that Jazz had. I wish I had a little of it. When she argued in class with Ms. Dennis over her views on Picasso, Ms. Dennis had changed her mind and agreed with Jazz. Said so in front of the class. Then there was her running cross-country on the boys' team, and beating most of them. There was no doubt in my mind that she would win and get the best of it. Whatever *it* was.

I picked up the van Gogh book and opened it randomly. John Mark had marked it up with a highlighter, so I read the first thing I saw. "He says that you should walk and love nature because it helps you understand art." I looked across at John Mark. "I totally agree with that. I walk every day, all the way to the train tracks. Van Gogh and I have something in common."

"If you walk that far, you should be running cross-country," Jazz said.

"No way," I replied.

"Here. My turn," Jazz said. She took the book from me, keeping her finger in it. She read the next marked portion and said, "He's an autumn freak. Sorry, but fall is too sad, with everything drying up, dying and freezing. Summer for me."

"Yeah," John Mark said, "swimming and no school."

"Fall is my favorite season," I said.

I closed my eyes, seeing the touchable light on the maple the week before. "I wrote a poem about it," I said.

"Read it," John Mark said.

I shook my head. I hadn't read my poems out loud to anyone before. What would they think?

"Come on," Jazz said. "I'll read mine." She opened a notebook and read, " 'Entering the door of thought.' " She stopped.

"That's it?" John Mark said. "One line?"

"No, of course not." Jazz grinned. "But it's all I have so far."

"Well, that's more than me," John Mark said. "Your turn, Jude."

I opened my notebook. It would probably look dumb if I didn't read now; it would become some huge thing.

> *"Change is stilled by a hush.*
> *The leaves are brushed with fluid light.*

They leave a shade of memory.
A clear-eyed touch for winter."

I closed my notebook with a thump, hoping it covered the pounding inside me. When I looked up, Jazz and John Mark were staring at me. My face heated up, and I went back to sketching.

"Mad good," Jazz said. I smiled my thanks.

John Mark said, "Superior. Choice!" He paused like he was going to go on.

"Enough," Jazz told John Mark. She looked at me and said, "I loved it. Really."

"Anyway," John Mark said, "I will go on to say what I was going to say before I was so rudely interrupted. I wish I was done with my poetry homework this week. And that's the most I've heard you say at one time." He grinned at me.

I realized he was right. We'd crossed some friendship line and I was still okay. Amazing. I started sketching again, but it wasn't the cook anymore. It was van Gogh's eyes. "I want to get this book and mark it up for myself. And it will help with my art paper. Anyone want to go to Borders?"

Jazz said, "Can't. I've got cross-country today and tomorrow."

"McDonald's, the great foundation of our national

economy, has called once again," John Mark said. "Sorry, I work today, but I could go tomorrow."

He glanced down at my sketchbook. Van Gogh's eyes stared up at him. "God, you are good!" He drew out the word *good* for emphasis. "They look just like these." He pointed to the cover of the van Gogh book.

"I have to visit my grandmother first," I said as I got into the car with John Mark the next afternoon after school. "Would you mind taking me to the Care Home on Main Street? It won't take long. Fifteen minutes or so."

"No problem," John Mark said. He drove me to the Care Home, but instead of waiting in the car, he opened the door and got out. I hadn't planned on this, and it surprised me. Most people avoid nursing homes. Queasiness rippled from my gut up. What would he think of my grandmother and my one-way conversations with her? Would they seem crazy to him? I couldn't exactly tell him to go back and sit in the car. He was doing me a favor.

As soon as John Mark stepped into the home, he gulped and held his breath. When he couldn't hold it any longer, he started breathing through his mouth. When we got to my grandmother's room, he stopped just inside the door and leaned against the wall. I knew he was watching me as I kissed my grandmother.

"It's good to see you. How are you today?" I said, and paused.

Same as always. I'm glad you're here. Who is your friend?

John Mark stared at me and then looked back at Gram when she didn't say anything out loud.

"Oh, I've brought my friend John Mark to meet you," I said, straightening the cover and tucking everything in. "He's in my poetry class, and we eat lunch together."

That's good. You don't need to clean so much, dear, although I do love how it looks when you're done. I hummed "Hey Jude" as I swept.

John Mark was quiet. He watched me as I walked over to the window ledge. I watered a plant, pulled off some dead leaves, and said, "This place can always use some cleaning, Gram. When we're done here, we're going to Borders to buy a book of van Gogh's letters. Wouldn't it be great if I could paint like him?"

That would be wonderful. I'm sure you can do anything you want, Jude.

John Mark scratched his shoulder. He cleared his throat. I hummed "Sergeant Pepper's Lonely Hearts Club Band" as I finished cleaning.

I straightened the turquoise chair, the tray table, and the pleats of the curtains. I stopped by the bed and squeezed the uncurled hand. No response, same as always. I said, "I'll be back tomorrow. Love you."

I'll be looking for you. I love you too.

As we drove to Borders, John Mark said, "Did she have a stroke?"

"Yeah," I answered.

"Do you think she can hear you?" I took a deep breath and focused on his hands on the steering wheel. Ten and two, just where they were supposed to be.

Steady voice. Just use a steady voice, I told myself. "Yes," I replied. "I'm sure of it." I breathed again. "A lot of research says that people in comas can hear you, so I'm sure stroke victims do too."

"Do you think she'll ever answer you?" John Mark asked.

"She hasn't yet. Not out loud, anyway, but I hear her answers in my mind," I said.

"I guess you know her real well, then."

"The first time I met her was when we moved here in July. She'd already had the stroke, but I know she's a good grandmother. Some things you just know deep inside," I said.

John Mark was quiet for a while, and then he said, "Yeah, I know what you mean. Are you a Beatles fan?"

"Yeah, that's about all I listen to," I said, and

stared out the window. John Mark had seen a piece of my world. There wasn't any going back. I should have thought through my request for a ride to the Care Home a little more. How could I have known he was going to come in? Maybe I could have seen it coming. He wasn't shy; he'd talked to me first. He was acting in the school play.

When we got to Borders, I found *Dear Theo* right away. John Mark brought us two big mugs of coffee while I sat at a table.

As we sipped the coffee, I read some of the letters, and John Mark looked through a giant book of van Gogh's paintings. "You've got me looking at his eyes now. It's freaky how the color of his eyes changes in the self-portraits," he said.

"Yeah. He wasn't into realism in that way. He used color to show something about himself. Cool, huh? Right now I'd paint your eyes green, which means new, because you want something different. Deep even, unlike almost everyone else at school." I paused, wanting to get the right words. "Under your 'great' intelligence, you have questions that no one has answered for you so far. At the Care Home, though, I'd have painted them soft, brown caramel. Sadness."

"You're scaring me, Jude. Are you psychic?" He paused. "No. It's more like you see into people.

Do you? No, don't tell me." John Mark looked down at the van Gogh book again and said, "I don't know about the color stuff, but the expression in his eyes doesn't change. He looks insecure, frightened— something." He took a deep sip of coffee, brushed his ponytail back over his shoulder, and looked at me.

"I think you're right," I said. I wondered what that said about me, identifying with van Gogh. Insecure, frightened? Yeah, at times maybe, but not all the time.

"You know a lot about van Gogh. Are you already working on your art paper?"

"Yeah. But this isn't just homework, John Mark. This is—oh God, what's the word?" I paused until it came to me. "Destiny. Destiny, that's it. His stuff makes me think and draw in ways I haven't before. His biography freaks me out."

"Why?" John Mark asked.

Why not just say it? I thought. He'd seen me listening to my grandmother; he probably thought I was at least a little nuts, but I hoped he didn't think I'd hack my ear off. "There are a lot of parallels between our lives."

John Mark watched as I began to sketch. "There's no doubt that you see like an artist. Look at how you draw."

"Thanks," I said. "You make it easy to talk, John Mark."

"I'm safe," he said. In a minute or so, van Gogh's eyes were staring at him from my sketchbook again. He looked at his watch. "Oh God, I have to get going. My family is getting together with Jazz's tonight."

"Your families know each other?"

"Jazz is my cousin."

"Oh," I said. Now I understood the closeness between them—a little, anyway. I don't have any cousins, so I could only imagine.

"Besides," he said, "I've had enough of those eyes." I bought the van Gogh book, and we drove back to E-ville, where I had him drop me off in the square instead of in front of our building. Seeing my grandmother was enough family for John Mark today. I wasn't ready for anyone to see Stella, or the crappy apartment.

"Where have you been, you bitch?" Stella yelled when I walked in. I looked at the ponytail on top of her head. It was shaking. That meant action. One hand had a cigarette in it, so I watched the other. My mother has never hit me, but she has thrown stuff around.

"Oh," Stella went on, "and there's your supper." She pointed to a plate on the table.

Why had she made supper? Stella rarely cooks. When I was little, Stella cooked more often. On special days like birthdays, I got to choose whatever I wanted, and she did her best to make it. It had been a long time since that happened. Now she mainly brings home the day-old or expired stuff from the convenience store. Any cooking got me wondering. Usually she did it when she felt guilty about something like who she was seeing or some dumb thing she'd done. Sort of like when I used to clean the bathroom after I'd stolen money or cigarettes from her purse.

She picked up the plate of macaroni and cheese, the boxed kind. The macaroni had brown congealed hardness on the edges. It looked like there were some wrinkled peas on the plate too. She tilted it sideways over the sink to spill out the food. Then she threw the plate in the sink, and it cracked when it hit the bottom.

"Oh shit," Stella said. Her voice dropped on the word *shit*. That was a good sign. It meant that her anger might fall apart. Like an old tire. If throwing the plate in the sink was the outer threads, then with any luck, the rest would disintegrate. I watched until the ponytail tilted sideways and then fell forward.

I didn't say a word. When her hair began slipping out of the scarf that tied it up, I decided it was safe to walk across the room. There'd be no flying objects at least. She put out her cigarette and picked up the pieces of the plate.

"I'm outta here. Don't worry about the dishes. Do the laundry, okay? If you don't get a babysitting job." Stella dropped the broken pieces of the plate into the trash can, grabbed her purse, and headed toward the door.

I wondered why she was feeling guilty. What was going on? Then I had it. It had to be the trucker she'd met at the bar. Buddha must have answered her prayers, and she was going to tell me about it. She was bringing him home. Was he moving in? I hoped not. The apartment was too small, and the walls were too thin.

I grabbed a bag of salt-and-vinegar chips. The sour taste suited my mood. I sat down on the brown-and-green plaid sofa and read some more of the biography. Then I started copying quotes from it into my sketchbook. With each quote, I'd draw the image that popped into my mind: leaves, eyes, tombstones. Spider-Man curled up beside me. I put on the Beatles.

The ache in my mind was spiking through my whole head. Had too much pain seeped out today, or was I letting too many people inside? Talking to John Mark had reminded me of the stupid things in my life that I couldn't change. It just made me feel more. More crap. I didn't know what to do with it.

I lay back on the couch. "Relax, relax," I said as I rubbed my temples, and then that small place at the back of my head, the one right at the bottom of my skull. But when I closed my eyes, the picture came. The one I'd seen so many times.

It had started out as a dream. I was in a white dress. I looked like a princess from the Middle Ages. I was standing in a clearing, looking up at the stars. I could feel water dripping on my feet, but when I looked down, I realized it wasn't water. It was blood dripping from my wrists. I'd woken up and thought, *Oh good, the blood oath is letting the pain drip away.* It felt good to let the pain out.

But the next time I had the dream, the blood was dripping both from my wrists and from my nose. I woke myself up and ran into the bathroom. My nose wasn't bleeding.

The last time I had the dream, the blood was seeping out of me, from my ears, and eyes, and it began to dribble down my mouth. I woke up screaming.

That dream showed me that the pain inside would kill me if it came out. Better to smother it and shut it up. I wouldn't let it into my conscious world. No one could live with that much pain. I didn't have the dream anymore, which was strange, but sometimes when I closed my eyes, I saw myself in the white dress.

I needed space. I wanted the wide dark air. I

needed the railroad tracks. I turned off my music and left the apartment. As I walked, I kept my eyes fixed on the stars. Some leaves crinkled under my feet. I heard a train's whistle and realized there was a freight train that went through late at night. That meant there was one in the afternoon and one at night. I looked at my watch. It was eleven thirty.

I waited for the eyes. The red train eyes had become van Gogh's eyes. I saw them. They were coming, coming. I focused on them, blanking out everything. Feeling nothing but the rush of adrenaline. I jumped off the tracks. When I got home, the pain was not so bad, but it was still there, and I was so tired. I hoped I could sleep.

Six

I didn't see Stella at all on Thursday, but when I walked into the kitchen on Friday morning, to my surprise there was a man sitting at the table. So Stella *had* been trying to tell me about a man earlier in the week, and she *was* feeling guilty.

He had on a wife beater T-shirt. Not a good sign. He was bald, but it looked like he was trying to make up for it with an incredibly long beard. It covered some of his beer belly. Considering all the hair on his chest and shoulders, I wasn't sure he needed a beard to make up for anything.

I headed for the fridge. I opened the door and was surprised to find a little jug of low-fat chocolate milk. I drank it down and turned to leave. The man stood up. He was huge. I almost jumped back but managed to keep my feet in place. He held his hand out to me. "I'm Lou. You must be Jude."

"Yes," I said. I shook his hand. I was surprised. Stella must have said something about me to him. I should have added *Pleased to meet you* to be polite, but I wasn't particularly pleased. Still, on the other hand, no other man of hers had taken the trouble to introduce himself.

When we lived in Memphis, I'd walked into the kitchen one morning to see a man with no shirt on. That wasn't unusual, but the Memphis man had a snake tattoo curling down his left arm toward a hand that held a doughnut. It looked like the snake was going after the doughnut.

I sat down across from him and pulled a doughnut out of the box between us. The man had already eaten five and was about to eat a sixth, which he did in two bites. With the first bite, part of the custard center spilled out and onto the table, and then he stuffed the second bite into his mouth. The custard sat on the table in shiny little heaps. I tried to eat half my doughnut in one bite, but it so filled my mouth that I thought I was going to choke. That night Stella told me his name was Stan, and I'd immediately said, "Stan, Stan the doughnut man," which Stella told me

I wasn't to say to him. It wasn't a big problem considering the snakes and all.

He never once spoke during the doughnut-eating ritual that took place every day he lived with us, and that was a number of months. I still don't know who bought the doughnuts every day. It must have been him. I stopped eating custard doughnuts after that first morning. I haven't eaten them since.

"Pleased to meet you," I said to Lou, the new man. "Heading out soon?" I hoped I wasn't being too obvious.

"Yes, I am. I'm going home for the weekend. We've got a place an hour or so north. Up along eleven looking over the river."

God, did that mean he had a wife at home? Not again. Stella had gone out with a married man who kept promising he would leave his wife and never did. Now she stuck with divorced or single men. I couldn't think of a thing to say. I nodded. He must have taken this as a good sign, because he went on.

"*We* means me and the two cats. They're my wife's cats. She died a year ago. The cats really haven't taken to me, but I can't give them away."

A widower, I thought. *Now, that is a change.* No wonder Stella was attaching to him as tight as a leech. A man who took care of his dead wife's cats sounded like a man who stuck with a woman. Could be a good thing. You never knew.

"Sorry to hear about your wife," I said.

"Well, thanks," he said. He sat back down and scratched his belly.

The door opened, and Stella breezed in with two coffees in Styrofoam cups. I was speechless. Stella hadn't "breezed in" in the morning in a long, long time. She had a plastic grocery bag over her arm. "I see you two have met," she said. She placed the coffees on the table, and Lou grabbed one. Poor man, it looked like he hadn't realized that Stella didn't even do coffee.

"Yes," I said. I didn't bother to hide the tight edge to my voice. The edge that said *You didn't even warn me this time.* Stella took a box of Krispy Kreme doughnuts out of the grocery bag.

"Help yourself," she said.

"No, thanks," I said, and headed for my room. I slid into the bathroom and took an incredibly fast shower. I didn't want to think about Lou, or cats, or the possibility of belly scratching or places on the river. Was Stella thinking of joining him at his place on the river? I couldn't imagine him moving into our apartment when he had his own place.

I almost ran out the door to school. I got there

earlier than usual and saw Todd pull into the parking lot as I was walking across it. Shy or not, it was time for him to ask me out again. Maybe I'd ask *him* if he didn't.

"Hey, Jude." He laughed and hummed a few bars of the Beatles song. "I bet you've gotten that a lot." I nodded.

"You want to go bowling tomorrow night?" he asked.

"Sure," I said, and then immediately wished I could take it back. I'd never been bowling in my life. But bowling or not, it was with Todd, and I wasn't going to turn down a chance to go out with him again.

That night I went to the football game by myself, which is something that no one does. Going alone and not knowing anything about the game had kept me away before E-ville, but I wanted to watch Todd and see if I could figure out something about the game before we went out again. Todd nodded at a man and woman on the upper bench before the game started. From the way the woman waved back, a jerky little flutter, I guessed they were his parents.

I nearly froze to death sitting on those metal bleachers. It was colder than usual. I never took my eyes off Todd, and I practiced telepathy by willing him to stay alive. I held my breath until he emerged from under every pile of bodies and stood up, giving a little shake of the shoulders that meant he was okay. The only thing I'd figured out about the game so far was that each side tried to get the ball down the field to the end and that the other side tried to stop them by piling on them. It was obvious — even to me — that Todd was really good. He threw the ball and ran a lot. People yelled, "Go, Todd" the whole time.

I huddled deeper in the old afghan I'd brought and stared at the cheerleaders. People who were cheerful and peppy in that cold had to be nonhuman. I decided that they were either humanoid aliens or cleverly disguised bloodless reptiles. That thought warmed me, but still I couldn't wait for the game to end. When it did, I ran all the way home.

When I got home, I put on the Beatles, sketched, and fell asleep with the CD playing.

On Saturday, Todd picked me up. I told him I lived in the block near the town square, and I waited for him down on the street. I jumped in the truck almost before he stopped. "Hi, Jude."

"Hi." I fiddled with the seat belt to cover my nervousness about my bowling, or should I say my lack of bowling.

"Do you go bowling a lot?" I asked.

"My dad was in a league when I was little, and he took me with him a lot. I love bowling."

Great, I thought. Better to just be honest. I cleared my throat. "Actually, I've never bowled before."

"No problem," Todd said. "You won't be that bad." One arm was stuck out the window, and with his other hand he turned on the radio. I didn't know the song, or the station for that matter. It was country. The pure stuff with steel guitars and nasal twangs. I'd never listened to one whole country song on the radio, but Stella did listen to Willie Nelson now and then. "On the Road Again," as you can imagine, was a particular favorite of hers.

Anyway, if Todd liked country music, there had to be something good about it. It did go with the truck. After the second sad song I didn't know, I was hoping for Willie, and "Always on My Mind." I secretly liked the song but had never let on to Stella. I considered it a classic, not just country. Then to my astonishment, Willie's voice filled the cab, singing that very song. Good luck or fate? Fate, I decided.

At the bowling alley, I watched the ball go down the gutter my first three times up. Todd scratched his head when he put our score in.

"Here, let me help you," he said. "You hold the ball like this." He balanced it on his chest. I did the same. "Then you bring your arm back like so." He arched his arm back. I did the same. Or so I thought, but Todd laughed and said, "No, not like that. I'll show you. Put your ball down."

He came over and stood right behind me, putting his arm under my right arm. He folded my hand up like we were holding a bowling ball and then pulled it back and swung it forward. I, of course, was not paying a bit of attention to bowling technique. All I could feel was the heat of his body against mine. As far as I was concerned, *this* was bowling.

"Go, Todd," the guy at the snack bar said. He whistled in the way you usually use your fingers for, only he didn't need his fingers. Clearly, he'd had lots of practice.

Todd stepped back immediately, and I almost stumbled. My face flamed up so hot, I was afraid sweat would break out on my forehead and upper lip. I'd die if it did. *Cool,* I thought, *just stay cool.* I wondered if Todd had the red streaks going up his neck. I turned to look at him, and sure enough, there they were.

Todd wiped sweat off his forehead and said, "It's hot in here." I just laughed, thankful it was him doing the sweating. "You want something to drink?" he asked.

"Sure," I said. I sat down while he went to get some sodas.

After he came back and we'd both had a few sips, I said, "I think I can do it now." I threw another perfect gutter ball. Todd kept trying to help me, but after a while it just gave me the giggles, so I told him to stop. I was hopeless. Todd bowled two hundred. I stopped looking at my score.

"You *are* consistent," Todd said. "Amazingly consistent."

"I'm just perfecting the gutter ball," I said. "That has to be the true purpose of the game, because no one would invent a game that messes up the perfect symmetry of the pins."

Todd stared at me and laughed again. "What is inside your head?"

I just smiled, the great response when you don't know what to do. I hoped he read it as a mysterious *Wouldn't you like to know?* and not as *I haven't a clue what to say.*

He must have taken it as mysterious, because when we pulled up on the street in front of the apartment, he kissed me, and it seemed like he wanted to know me more. I sure wanted something between us. When we broke apart five minutes later, I knew he had the idea.

"I'll be calling you, Jude," he said as I got out of the truck. As I walked toward the apartment, I could feel his eyes on my back or butt; I'd take either one.

Seven

That Monday at lunch, John Mark came up to the table. I was reading van Gogh's letters. "Have a seat," I said without looking up.

He didn't. He stood there until I looked at him. His hair was pulled up under a straw hat. His face was blank. He shrugged and held both his hands palms up as if asking a question and said, "Our inward thoughts, do they ever show outwardly? There may be a great fire in our soul, and no one ever comes to warm himself at it."

"You are good!" I said. "Sit down and tell me your inward thoughts, van Gogh."

John Mark sat down. "Did you know that quote?" He pulled a card out of his pocket and showed it to me. On the card was the quote. John Mark had gotten the part of Romeo in the school play. He was always spouting off stuff he'd memorized. He really wanted to be an actor.

"No, it was the hat. Tipped me off."

"What did you do over the weekend?" Jazz asked when she came over and sat down across from me.

"I went to the football game."

"Hello? You went to the football game?" Her voice rose.

"You don't seem like the football type," John Mark said as he pulled out a sandwich. He opened it up and stuffed it with potato chips. I kept my eyes on the sandwich because I was blushing and annoyed.

"I'm learning about the game," I said.

"Why?" Jazz said. Then she tapped her temple with her index finger. "Ah, I get it." She switched into her Yoda voice and wrinkled her face, squinching up her nose. "Wise, I am."

John Mark said, "Tell me more."

Jazz said, "Todd. Pizza City, hmmm," in the same Yoda voice.

I looked back down at my book. "Excuse me, I am reading here."

"And?" Jazz said.

"And what?" I answered.

"And what did you do Saturday night?" Jazz said.

"I went bowling with him. And what were you guys doing?" I stuffed a handful of chips in my mouth.

"I was with my older sister, who's back from Penn State for the weekend," Jazz said. "We went shopping. But to get back to a more interesting subject, I'll just pose a hypothetical question. Why is it that girls always go for the least likely person? Is it the opposites thing, the romantic ideal thing or what? Any ideas, anyone?"

I blushed. I hated the way my own face betrayed me. I didn't know the answer to the opposites thing, but I didn't see anything wrong with dreaming of the ideal. Why would I want to date someone like me? Jazz was waiting, but I wasn't about to answer. I doodled.

"I'm not touching that question," John Mark said, "but while you"—he pointed at Jazz—"were shopping, and you"—he pointed at me—"were bowling, I was slaving away at McDonald's. Is my life sad or what?"

Jazz laughed. She has this loud, low laugh. It seems funny coming out of her small body. It makes me wonder where she keeps it. "Poor boy," she said. "I'm going out to Hess's after school today. I'm skipping cross-country. Either of you want to come along?"

"Can't. I've got to"—John Mark stopped and made a groaning sound—"work."

"How sad," Jazz said, sarcastic pity dripping

from her voice, "your life is so hard. Nobody else has to work."

"Hess, like your last name?" I asked. "What's that?"

"It's one of my favorite places. How about I take you there after school?"

"After I see my gram. I'll meet you in the square at four thirty, okay?"

"Okay."

Jazz was early. She had her mother's banged-up hundred-year-old station wagon. It actually had wooden side panels. We drove out of Ellenville and down a road with rolling fields on either side. On the left, at the far edge of the fields, there was a ridge of trees. They were starting to turn yellow, red, and orange. We turned on a little dirt road and parked near the small cemetery at the end. Tall pines and other trees stood on three sides of it. A lot of the stones looked really old. Some leaned back, and some were half-sunken.

"Welcome to Hess's," Jazz said.

"Peaceful," I said.

"Yeah," Jazz said. "Nobody bothers you here."

"I've always liked cemeteries."

"In the spring I saw a whole family of eastern bluebirds in that tree." Jazz pointed to a big sycamore at the edge of the cemetery.

"I don't know if I've ever seen a bluebird," I said, sitting on the ground. "Did you know that van Gogh liked cemeteries?"

"Doesn't surprise me somehow. Knowing van Gogh's life, he was probably thinking about death. But this place reminds me of life."

"How?" I asked. I was picking clover, looking for a four-leafed one.

"The way it continues. Generation after generation. You can see grandparents and their grandchildren here. The oldest stone in this place goes all the way back to 1770. It's on Michael Hess's grave. And look at all the Hesses that followed him."

"Are these people really your ancestors?"

"Yeah," Jazz said. "A lot of them. My family's lived around here for two hundred years."

We walked around, looking at her family stones. "It seems impossible," I said. "I can't imagine a history, a home, and all that family stuff. It sounds so grounded, settled."

Jazz laughed.

"What's so funny?" I said.

Jazz waved her arm across the cemetery. "Yeah, this looks pretty grounded and settled to me." I laughed too.

"It just seems funny," Jazz went on, "because I've spent half my life wishing I could get away from here and all the family stuff. Don't get me wrong: I think roots are okay, and I love my family, but the expectations that people can have of you! And the comparisons that people make when your family has always lived somewhere. If I hear one more 'Your sister was . . .' or even 'Your father was . . .' I think I'll puke! Some of the teachers in our school taught my father. Can you believe that? I am so unlike my sister or my father, it's unbelievable. It's so stifling. Especially when you don't fit the family norm."

"And you don't?" I said.

"Hardly," Jazz answered. "Do I seem like a genius? God, listen to me. Blah, blah, blah. But you said you can't imagine family stuff?"

"Yeah, I thought things would be different here in Ellenville with family stuff, but they aren't. I mean we moved here to be with my grandmother, but she'd had a stroke and isn't doing too well. She's all the family I've got besides my mother." *Who hardly counts,* I thought. I lay down with my hands under my head.

Jazz sat down beside me. "What about your mother?"

I felt the old clutch/choke in my throat, but when I stopped to breathe slowly, I thought, *Well, she did tell me some of her stuff,* so I guessed I could tell her some of mine. She probably figured out things weren't that great from our discussion in the art museum about crazy van Gogh eyes.

"Stella? She's hopeless, and she won't change."

"What do you mean?" Jazz said.

I paused and closed my eyes. I didn't want to see if there was pity in hers. "She works at convenience stores, she drinks, and she picks up men in bars. Always hoping that the next one in the next place will be permanent. All the moves and nothing has changed. That's her life. I don't want to be like her." White dots chased around the back of my eyelids. It was like REM sleep movement, only I was awake. I opened my eyes.

The look on Jazz's face was thoughtful, not pitying. I was glad. "I don't think you will be," she said. "Maybe you can't change her, but you could change other things."

"Hasn't happened so far," I said. "Besides, what if things are just inevitable?" *Like hearing the train coming but not being able to get out of the way.*

We were silent for a while as we watched the inflated clouds shift and shape.

"That's too hopeless," Jazz said.

"But hope can be mean," I went on. "If it dies, which it always does, and you hope again, it's brutal.

Then you just die another life. Like a damn cat."
And I've already used up eight of my lives. I've only got one left.

"Hope can't be all mean," Jazz said. "It gets too many people through the crap in life. Hope is about the good stuff that we don't always see, don't you think? There's got to be more than what I know so far, and I mean to find it! Anyway, I still think something *could* change for you."

Maybe she was right about hope. I wanted to believe there was something more than I could see, even did sometimes, but stuff happened and sucked all the good away. And pain remained. I got up and went to a different part of the cemetery. And maybe Jazz was right about there being more than what we knew. She was convincing. But change for me? I doubted it.

"I love reading the stones," I said. "Can you imagine all of a life summed up in two lines? Actually, that wouldn't be too hard for me, but for you!" I looked at her.

"Impossible to do," Jazz said. "I'm into too much."

"Have you seen this stone? It's my favorite so far. Mary Conrad. Died July 23, 1873. Age sixteen years, two months. I wonder what her story was. Just a little younger than me. I wonder if she killed herself."

"She probably died of a disease. Nobody lived too long back then." Jazz came over to Mary's stone and sat down beside me. "Why would you say she killed herself?"

I kept staring at the stone. "Life was hard back then," I said. "People killed themselves. Just like today. Lots of high-school kids think about suicide. I read that one in five kids thinks seriously about it." I pulled up a stray dandelion.

"I never have. Even when life is crappy. There is so much I still want to do."

"And you don't ever doubt that you will, do you?"

"No," she answered. We were watching the clouds. It was that quiet sort of comfortable. Jazz is the kind of person you can say things to, or not say things to, without having to think too much. A good person to have as a friend. Was she a friend? It seemed so.

"This is a good place, Jazz. Thanks for bringing me."

"Thanks for sharing it," she said. "I knew you'd like it too."

We drove back into town, and Jazz dropped me off at the square.

That Wednesday in art, Ms. Dennis headed over to my table. Over the weeks, I'd noticed that though her comments about people's artwork were true, they were never put-downs. Not as honest as I would have been, but they did make you think. It's like there wasn't a "right way" to do things, but you wanted to do more. Most everyone really worked at stuff, which was truly amazing in a high-school class, much less in an art class. She didn't just glance; she stopped and studied my work.

Maybe it was because everyone else was drawing, and I was painting. Yellow. Just yellow.

Ms. Dennis's pause was longer than usual. I could smell her musk scent. It wasn't just musk; it was vanilla musk. I shifted in my seat and leaned closer to my desk, which caused it to squeak, but nobody looked. Everyone was busy working on their own drawing projects.

We'd finished pottery a week ago, and everyone was spread out. Todd was on the other side of the room. I missed the brush of his arm against mine, the glances and occasional comments. I wanted to be next to him every day, but I liked painting so much better than pottery.

We were supposed to be drawing the same object from different perspectives. We only had to turn in two pictures, but I was on my third. I'd have to move on to a different object at this rate.

"Chairs," Ms. Dennis said. "I like that, but they're supposed to be from different angles. We're working on depth."

"You used the word *perspective,*" I said. I pointed

to the picture at the top of my table. It was pretty straightforward. A chair with a cane seat. "So I used that word for this project. I call it *Perspectives of Reality*. This one is the chair as most people see it, *Reality One*."

"The obvious," Ms. Dennis said. "It looks like van Gogh's chair, the one he painted in his house in Arles after Gauguin left." *Hey, she's good,* I thought, and darted a quick look up at her; she was staring at the picture. Her steely, corkscrew curls massed forward around her face. I nodded.

"And this one?" Ms. Dennis tapped the second picture with her finger, making the bangles slip down her arm with a jangly sound.

"That's reality as it is, constantly shifting. *Reality Two*." In this picture, the same chair was in a corner of the art room. The walls with their posters of artists bulged inward, and the floor slanted toward the chair.

Ms. Dennis nodded, and her long earrings made a tinkling sound as the moon and stars clinked together. "Things look different from the chair's perspective," she said. I nodded.

"And this last picture is ultimate reality. *Reality Three*." I pointed to my yellow sheet. "The true chair, molecules of energy." I wondered if Ms. Dennis would see that there was more to the pictures than met the eye. Not everyone would.

87

For this project, I'd created three worlds to portray reality. There was the obvious reality, which everyone sees and assumes they know. Then there was a shifting reality, like my different lives: the carefully suppressed pain life—my "family" and my past; my escapist life in my art, walks, and dreams; and the obvious school life. And finally in my last picture, what I've dreamed of: a timeless reality full of something cosmic. Lots of light and energy. God, it sounds impossible, but sometimes when I paint, I think I catch glimpses of it.

Ms. Dennis didn't say anything. I thought she was going to move on. But when I didn't hear a jangle, I looked up.

"You've put a lot of thought into this project, Jude. It has a lot of layers. Like life." She'd gotten it!

"Yeah," I said.

"Doesn't yellow mean happiness for van Gogh?" she asked.

"It does," I said, keeping my eyes down on the picture.

"Do you have any free time today?" Ms. Dennis said.

"Yes," I said. "I have a study hall after lunch."

"Great," Ms. Dennis said. "Stop by. We can talk about your work."

•   •   •

After lunch, I opened the door and peeked in the art room. Ms. Dennis was at the big sink washing her hands. "Oh hi, Jude," she said. "Come on in. Just cleaning up."

I walked in and sat down. I poked a finger through the hole in the hem of my black *Star Wars* T-shirt. It was amazing the shirt held together at all, it was so old. When I was little, it was one of my two gigantic sleeping T-shirts. One had Princess Leia's face on it, and the other had Chewbacca's. The T-shirts weren't big anymore, and I didn't wear them for sleeping. I wore them when I needed the Force.

"You know, we've been in school for a while now," Ms. Dennis said, "and I never heard you say as much as you did today."

"Yeah," I said. "I'm not into pottery." I jiggled the toe of my boot on the floor.

"Seems like drawing and painting are more your things," Ms. Dennis said. I nodded. "What gave you the idea for the paintings?"

I wasn't about to say *my shitty life*. I liked her, and maybe she had seen a lot, but who knew what a teacher would do? Maybe she would feel like she had to refer me to some learning psychologist or something. I'd already been through that at another school. I didn't want anybody else telling me what they thought about my life. I pulled the van Gogh letters book out of my backpack and said, "This book."

"Tell me about it," she said.

"He says that showing things differently, even incorrectly, can reveal deeper truths about them. I think he was always trying to do that."

"And you do the same thing in your work—reveal things. I guess life, maybe even people, aren't always what they seem." She stopped and I didn't say anything, so she went on.

"Are you doing van Gogh for your research paper?"

"Yeah. His work is great."

Ms. Dennis said, "You're very talented. I'd like to see you be able to do more in art. You're a senior, aren't you?"

I nodded. This was beginning to sound like one of those "potential" conversations that I didn't like, but because she had gotten my paintings, I didn't turn her off immediately. "Have you thought about going to college or art school of some kind?" she asked.

What was the sense of thinking about college? I had no money. I looked down and poked my finger in and out of the hole of my shirt. "No." Discouragement settled on me like the long shawls Ms. Dennis occasionally wore. It covered my shoulders, my heart. She was nice, but how long would she be around?

"Well, I'll get some information for you. You still have lots of time before next fall."

"Thanks," I said. I picked up my backpack and walked toward the door.

I went out to the cross-country course to watch Jazz compete. She came in second. "God, you're good," I said as we walked toward her house after the meet. "You must be so disciplined."

"I don't think of it that way," Jazz said. "I started running at the beginning of ninth grade. I'd get home from school and just take off. I started running to get away from everything, all the stupid people and groups at school, a stupid relationship I was in. I mean I was with a guy that I didn't even like just because he was cool. Is that stupid or what? God, I was so into all that crap. So I ran over rocks, tree stumps, miles of blacktop. Getting my frustrations out. I'd think about my life and the bad stuff that happened, my dad getting laid off, my sister getting sick—I mean she's okay now, but she wasn't. And then one day I realized I was just looking forward to the run. Period. I wasn't running away from anything, I was running into something. Feeling really alive." She groaned as she bent over and massaged her right calf. "But right now my leg is feeling too alive."

What would it be like to be really good at one thing? The thought picked at my brain later as I walked toward the Care Home, like a crow picking at roadkill. Could I be that good at art? In my mind I saw the crow peck out the eyes of a flattened rodent. No, not possible. I liked to draw, it was my other world, but that was it. I headed toward the Care Home.

Eight

On Friday night I went to Todd's game. Afterward, he
took me to Pizza City. We were waiting to get seated
when a bunch of the other football players showed up.
I realized it was the place to go in E-ville after games.

"Hey, Todd," Kevin Roberts said. He was a beefy
six-foot-one senior. He hit Todd on the back. "To the
big table." There was a girl with him, but I didn't
know her name, and Kevin didn't introduce her.

Todd glanced at me, checking that it was okay. I
just nodded. I didn't really know what it would mean.
Maybe it was some kind of football players' thing.

We followed Kevin to a big circular table in the
middle of the restaurant, where some other guys were

already sitting. Then the door opened and more football players came in and joined us.

"That last run was great, Todd," Kevin said. "We needed that touchdown. Was there a scout up there in the crowd? Somebody from Penn State maybe?"

Todd looked down and laughed a little. "I don't know. I was just looking out for that Mawser."

"Yeah," said Tim Novak. Novak changed his voice, and said, "Folks, we can see that the boy from Central, Brian Mawser, can tackle." He went on in the same voice like he was some kind of television guy announcing a game. Play after play. I couldn't believe it.

Todd leaned forward in his chair. He didn't say anything, but everyone else kept jumping in using their commentator voices. It got louder and louder. So this was the ritual.

Todd nodded now and then, but mostly he just ate. The unnamed girl smiled at me. The lights made her teeth look green. After he'd eaten a whole pizza, Todd looked at me and then said to everyone else, "Well, I got to get going. Milking in the morning." I was relieved.

"Thank God I'm not a farmer," Novak said. "I milked one summer and that was enough. No four a.m. jobs for me."

"See you, Todd," Kevin said when we got to the door. Todd just waved.

As soon as we started driving, I put the window down and gulped the cold air. Todd said, "Hey, I'm freezing." He put the window up and pulled me over to sit beside him.

After a minute or two, I put my head on his shoulder. We drove to the town parking lot behind our apartment. We kissed and then Todd broke away, too soon for me. I liked the flush in my whole body. He said, "I really do have to get going—four is early. How about if I pick you up tomorrow evening? After milking, say around six thirty? I have something special to show you, and then we could see a movie."

I went upstairs and lay on my bed thinking about those words: "something special." What could they mean? A thing? A person? A place? Whatever they meant, they were meant for me. Me, Jude Barnes. God, I loved those words: "something special." They sounded so good! I kept feeling the heat in my body as I remembered our kiss. Usually I want to fall asleep, but that night I didn't. Spider-Man jumped up on my bed, and I just kept saying the words "something special" out loud until finally they sounded silly. I ended up laughing and then just stroking Spider-Man.

The next evening, Todd picked me up, and we started driving out of town.

"Where are we going?" I asked.

"I want you to see my farm. It's been in the family for a hundred and fifty years."

A hundred and fifty years? That was, like, eternal. I couldn't wait to see it. This *was* something special. He was inviting me to see his family. It was what I'd dreamed about when I thought of the "ideal" man.

"My grandmother is my only family," I said.

"Oh yeah? Where does she live?"

"Here in E-ville. She's the reason we moved here. She had a stroke, and she's in the Care Home."

"Oh," Todd said. "I'm sorry."

"I go see her just about every day."

"You must love her," Todd said.

"I do."

Fields of dry corn alternated with fields of dark brown earth where a few broken cornstalks had survived the harvester. The trees along the road were mostly yellow and scarlet.

"My grandparents live about a mile from our place," Todd said. "My grandfather still milks cows, and my grandmother cooks all the big family meals — Thanksgiving, Christmas, Easter."

"That's cool," I said. *Unbelievable,* I thought. I pictured a Norman Rockwell painting I'd seen with all these people sitting around a table. I inserted myself into the picture.

"I guess it is. I never really thought about it

before. They've always been there." I felt this little twinge in my chest. Was it jealousy? Could jealousy really make you feel this physical thing? I couldn't imagine taking grandparents for granted. He didn't know how good he had it.

We pulled up onto a little ridge and stopped. Looking down from the hill, we could see a huge stone house with massive chimneys at either end. Two immense maples were flaming orange on the front lawn, which looked like it was ten acres. In back of the house were flower beds, trees, and stones in an immense landscaped garden. A huge white barn and three blue silos stood behind it. Everything was scrubbed! The place looked like a postcard.

"It's beautiful." I sucked in my breath. My eyes got glazy. I wanted it. I wanted it all so bad my ribs ached, or maybe it was my lungs? I couldn't tell for sure, but I knew that something hurt inside. I crossed my arms across my chest. I saw myself out there planting flowers in the garden, not that I'd even pulled a weed before, but I'd never had a chance. I saw kids running around. My kids, little kids chasing each other, laughing. Todd was standing behind me, and he put his arms around my waist. I couldn't imagine being from somewhere like this.

"My brother will live in the house, because he's going to take over the milking, but I plan to build a house on a couple of acres after I get done with college." We walked back to the truck and rode down beside the house and then went to the end of the road and turned left at the corner. We drove along through a stand of trees, and then Todd stopped and got out. The sun was going down. I followed him.

We were looking out over a field with a stream winding through it. "Right over there," he said, pointing to the other side of the stream. His voice had deepened, and his face was a dark red, not the mottled red of embarrassment. "That's where my house will be." The air was moist, soft, full of turned-up earth.

"Come on," he said. He grabbed my hand, and we walked along the stream. Goldenrod and chicory and some blue asters grew along the creek. We stopped at a place where the creek widened and there was a bunch of bulrushes. Todd dropped my hand, bent down, and picked up a few stones, then threw them at a tree on the other side of the creek.

"Did you play here a lot when you were little?" I asked.

"All the time. My mom says I have the record for 'accidentally' falling into the creek." He pointed to a tree in front of us. "See those boards up there? That's my old tree house." I could see a platform of sorts. "And over there in that pasture"—he pointed in the opposite direction—"is where I broke my arm horse-back riding."

I touched a bulrush, and then another and another. I rubbed the downy brown heads. Then I picked a plant with some curly dark green leaves and a purple flower spike at the top. It smelled like spearmint. As I held it to my nose, its scent overpowered all the other smells. It was an ancient moment, and I shivered as the coolness of the creek rose up and misted around me.

Todd pulled me into his arms and kissed me hard. I tingled from my scalp down. I kissed him right back. This was my ninth life. I could see it. Todd could pull me out of my old life and plant me in a new one. His.

"Hey, there." I jumped back. A guy was waving from the ridge. From a distance, he looked a lot like Todd. "Enjoying the view?"

"That's my brother," Todd said. He yelled, "Steve, meet Jude."

"Nice to meet you, Jude," Steve yelled.

I waved and pressed my other hand against my cheek to cool it off. God, what a mood breaker. I glanced at my watch. "It's almost time for the movie. We better get going."

Later that night, after the movie, we sat at the

Landon Diner, an all-night truck stop, and ate French fries.

"You know," I said, "I've never really understood it before."

"What?" Todd said.

"That whole 'love of the land' thing. I mean I've read about it in pioneer books, but when I saw your place and everything, I felt it."

Todd nodded. "Yeah, there must be something to that. It's always been a part of me. I mean, it would kill my dad if he thought he would lose the farm. And if something happened to Steve, I'd take over."

He looked down and drew circles in his catsup with a French fry. He was talking about deep stuff. I took a quick breath. This meant something good. I was sure of it. The tiny hairs on my forearms stood up, and I crossed my fingers in my lap under the table. Just for luck.

Stella was gone when I got home; she was working nights this week. When she worked days and I got home late enough in the evening, which I usually did after the tracks and the Care Home, she was already gone—out with Lou probably. He seemed to be in town a lot. Interestingly enough, they usually didn't come to our place.

Maybe he figured our apartment was too small for a big-bodied hairy man and two women. I didn't spend a lot of time thinking about him. He probably wouldn't be around too long. Stella left me notes telling me what she wanted me to do, and that was about it. It's amazing how well you can get along with someone you never see.

I turned in my van Gogh paper that Wednesday. It was early, but I felt good about it and wanted Ms. Dennis to read it. During lunches John Mark, Jazz, and I talked about van Gogh, poetry, acting, painting, and the little bits of life left over after those subjects. I didn't talk about Todd. It seemed that there was this place that I didn't want to go with John Mark or Jazz, even though I'd shared some deeper things with them.

We walked home together after school. I'd been in school for seven weeks. It seemed like a long time, but at the same time, it felt like things were going so fast. In fact, they seemed to be speeding up. I can't explain it. I'd never felt this heightened sense before. It was like my life was a movie and I was watching it with special 3-D glasses on. Every impression was sharpened.

"I'm going up on the tracks," I told Jazz and John Mark. I expected them to turn off, but instead they stayed with me and we walked along the tracks together. The air was filmy, like haze in summer.

We passed a silvery blue Volkswagen Beetle. "What a car. A classic," John Mark said. He placed his hands together in a praying mode and bowed toward it. "The newer Volkswagens can't touch that old model. They break all the time."

The sumacs on the hill along the track were brilliant red sprays among the dark fir trees. We walked to the rock formation, but we didn't climb up to the ledge. It might have been too small for all three of us. Instead we sat under a tree beside the rocks.

"This is a cool place," John Mark said as he tried to pick a Queen Anne's lace. The whole plant came up in his hand. We all laughed and settled back. The smell of chocolate permeated the air.

I wouldn't have thought it before, but the move to E-ville half convinced me that you can have too much of a good thing in chocolate. On the humid days, the smell is so thick I almost suffocate in it.

"I like it here," Jazz said. "I don't know why I never found this place before."

"Do you ever run on railroad tracks?" John Mark asked.

"Nope, too bumpy," Jazz answered.

"That's why," John Mark said.

"I come here nearly every day after school," I told them. "I climb up there"—I pointed to the ledge—

"and watch the freight train come. If I stay long enough, the Amtrak train goes by too."

"Why do you come here so much?" John Mark asked.

"Why not?" I said. "I like trains. Their headlights are eyes. Van Gogh's eyes. Watching them gives me focus, helps with the mind-ache."

"Do you mean headaches?" Jazz asked. "My mom gets migraines."

"No. It's different. It *can* be real pain, but sometimes it's a rushing noise or a jolt of glare. Like a snake that twists its way through the wrinkles in the gray stuff."

"The rushing, jolt stuff sounds like being hyper to me," John Mark said. "Like your brain is working really fast."

"No, that's not it, because sometimes it's just a piece of sadness. God, it's hard to explain. Sometimes it seems like a permanent grief. Who knows what for? I've had it since I was little, but it's been worse the last three years."

"Is the mind-ache what you were talking about when you looked at the van Gogh paintings in the museum?" Jazz said.

"Sort of."

"Does it ever go away?" Jazz asked.

"It lets up at times," I said. "The last week or so hasn't been as bad, but who knows?" I shrugged.

John Mark's silence irritated me. Like he was never sad or something. I said, "Everyone is really sad sometimes." They were both quiet, so I went on: "I don't mean my life is so hard, wah-wah, I couldn't get the dress I wanted at the mall or I broke my fingernail stuff, none of that it's-popular-to-be-depressed junk." I pulled my knees up, hooked my arms, and leaned my head on my knees. "I mean the godawful hollow that comes when you finally realize that something is lost forever. Like permanently gone and there's not a damn thing you can do to change it. There's a sucking whirlpool inside where something really fine used to be."

They were both quiet for a while. Then Jazz said, "Yeah, I know what you mean." She really knew what I was talking about. Something about the wrinkle in her forehead between her eyes told me so.

And then John Mark added, "You're right. Everyone does feel really sad at some point."

"It's no big deal," I said. But wasn't there a difference between feeling sad sometime and permanent grief? If so, I wasn't sure what it was or when you crossed from one into the other. Maybe there was a line somewhere that everyone knew about. Everyone but me.

I looked down at the sketchbook in my lap. I was drawing a crow. I remembered all the crows that van Gogh drew, and I pointed to one sitting in a tree only twenty feet away across the tracks. "I think we're on his turf. He's been yelling at me."

We got up, and Jazz and John Mark went back in town toward their houses. I went to see Gram, and then I headed back to the apartment.

After supper, I did the dishes that had been sitting in the coffee-stained porcelain sink for a couple of days. Stella had been sick with some kind of flu, which was unusual. When I'd looked in her bedroom the day before, she'd said, "Stay out, kid. I don't want you to get this too," and she'd waved one hand in a shooing motion.

So I left her alone. I listened to the Beatles while I waited for Todd's phone call. I didn't wait too long. He called often, but I never called his house. Once when I tried, his mother said, "Jude who?" and when I said, "Jude Barnes," she said, "He's real busy now. I'll tell him you called."

His mom knew everyone in town because they'd lived there forever, and the town wasn't that big. She probably thought that not knowing my name wasn't a good sign. Or maybe Todd had said something about me, and she wasn't too excited about it. When he didn't call back, I knew she hadn't said anything. She probably just didn't acknowledge unpleasant things. Like girls who weren't good enough. I could imagine her coughing politely and asking a new question whenever the talk strayed from the weather or the neighbors.

I'd never been to Todd's house, but then I didn't invite him to my house either. It was a case of the two worlds, Venus and Neptune, not being too close. He could wait to meet Stella. I didn't want to push it. I just couldn't take the chance that she could somehow, in some way, screw things up for me.

Nine

That Saturday morning, I went up to the ledge by the railroad tracks. I sat down, pulled out my sketchbook, and studied the cover. "Pretty good *Starry Night,* if I do say so myself," I said to the robin who thought the rocks were his. The crow was watching me too. I opened the sketchbook and read the first van Gogh quote I'd written. It said that art could keep you from feeling truly alone.

It had sounded good when I'd first read it, but it hadn't kept Vincent from being alone. He had needed someone to believe in him. Someone to love him. I had finished reading his biography a couple of nights before, and the story of his slow, agonizing suicide had stayed with me. If I closed my eyes and pictured one of his self-portraits with his pinched face and piercing eyes, I felt an instantaneous smarting behind my eyes.

I stood up and said to the robin, "But at least I'm not alone." I had Gram and Todd. And then there were Jazz and John Mark. They were friends, but friends were temporary. Who knew how long they'd be around? Todd was my best hope. He was the one who could give me a home.

A passenger train came toward me and stopped at the station. It started again and slowly moved past me. I waved as it picked up speed. *Good-bye, red eyes,* I thought. Life was good right now. Since that first date with Todd three weeks earlier, I'd been wrapped in a time warp. I wasn't going to let it stop. I wouldn't let anything mess things up. I headed toward the Care Home.

"Hi, Gram." I crossed to the bed and kissed her. "Did you know that van Gogh committed suicide? He felt so alone." I looked at my grandmother's open eye.

Being alone is a terrible thing. I know.

I worked on the plants. "In the end, he had no family, money, friends, or understanding from the art world. I think he thought nothing would change."

It sounds like he had too many things going against

him. When that happens, it is overwhelming. My eyes teared when I looked at her. I began sweeping.

"I think a lot of people feel that no one understands who they are or what they need. Did you ever feel that way?" I stopped sweeping.

Yes, I have. But you don't need to feel that way.

"You have me now, and I have you." I finished cleaning the sink and said, "I'll see you tomorrow. I love you."

I love you too.

In the afternoon Todd and I hiked up to Cherith Rock. It was a lookout place, where you could see up and down the Susquanita River. The sunset was layers of colors piled on top of one another. There was a gold layer, with turquoise on top of that and indigo on top of that. Above the colors, the moon rose and reigned supreme, with its white round face. While we were up there, I told Todd about my grandmother: how it really was, how she didn't talk, how important she was to me. He put his arm around me and he listened without saying anything, staring down at the river.

When I stopped talking, he gave me a paperback book on van Gogh that he had in his backpack. It was published by Taschen and had a self-portrait on the front. I held it with both hands to keep from hugging it to my chest. He had really listened to me, and he knew what was important to me. I mattered to him. God, it was sweet.

The next Wednesday, Jazz and I walked home after school. We went along the tracks together.

"You haven't said anything about Todd lately," Jazz said. "I suppose that's because I haven't asked." People in school knew about us, even though we weren't together outside of art class. A couple of visits to Pizza City on Friday nights, and word would have gotten around.

"That's true; you haven't. So before you can ask anything now, I do like him, and if you remember our conversation at the Art Museum, I said that maybe he was shy, and for the record, I was right. He's shy and sweet."

Jazz shook her head. "Are you infatuated or what? You might be right about the nice, shy, and all, but remember, smart girls can make bad choices when it comes to men." She paused. "God, that's good, isn't it? Sounds like a book or something. I can see it, my first book. I'll be on *Oprah*."

I stood up and cupped my hands around my mouth like I was yelling a long distance. "Come back from *Oprah*, Jazz." I sat back down. "The *right* smart girl can make all the difference in a guy's life."

"Guy?" Jazz said. "We're talking about boys here, and boys aren't into commitment. I mean, everyone says it, and it sure seems true to me."

I just laughed. "Yeah, right—you just haven't gotten over your ninth-grade screwup. Must have been bad."

She shrugged, and I looked away, but her words bothered me. Of course Todd was into commitment. Wasn't he? Look at his family, the farm. He cared deeply about things. He cared deeply about me. We could make things work.

We went to Jazz's house to get something to eat. When we walked in, I could smell cookies. Her mom was baking in the kitchen. I couldn't believe it. A cookie-baking mom. "It's good to meet you, Jude," she said. "Jazz has talked about you a lot. She says you're really good at art." I glanced at Jazz, and she was grinning.

"Well, I don't know if I'm good, but I like art."

"Come on, Jude, you're the best," Jazz said.

Her mom laughed. "Come over anytime, Jude. There's always plenty of food. I love baking."

"You wouldn't know it by looking at Jazz," I said.

"It's all that crazy running," her mom said. "Well, I've got to get the laundry." She walked out of the kitchen. I couldn't help staring after her. She did laundry? Home wrapped itself around me, sitting there in

Jazz's house. I saw, tasted, touched, and smelled it. Could you make home? Seemed like it. I vowed to be just like Jazz's mom someday. Of course, she'd have to give me some lessons.

On the walk home from school on Thursday, the leaves were swirling in a light wind. It was warm. I thanked the summer god.

When I got to the signal light, I didn't immediately head up to the rocks. I walked through the tunnel that started at the little train station and went under the tracks to a road on the other side. The sun poured down on me when I emerged. This sunlight was Vincent's color, pale lemon gold. I picked up a leaf, twirled it around, and offered it to a crow who was watching me. He didn't take it.

My van Gogh paper was in my backpack. I'd gotten it back the day before, but I hadn't looked at it yet. I'd been afraid. That afternoon I felt good. I was ready. The Mona Lisa had graded it in just a week. *The Mona Lisa* was John Mark's name for Ms. Dennis. He had names for every teacher; *the Mona Lisa* was one of the nicer ones.

I pulled my hair out of the rubber band and let it fall around my face. I looked for split ends, but there weren't many, so I separated some hair into tiny strands and braided them. I saw a little white aster and picked it. I stuck the flower in the braid and decided that the next week I'd dye my hair copper, pure penny copper. I was tired of black.

The freight train was coming. This one had two cars that looked like the same tagger had done them. I'd never seen this kind of graffiti. Green on black and yellow on red—great contrasts. Inside the giant words THE EYES ARE ON YOU! were little faces with round eyes. Some of the eyes were bloodshot, some had slanted eyebrows and squint lines, and some had glasses. The words or letters IOU, EOY, I IS, and EYE IS covered the rest of the car. I quickly pulled out my sketchbook and began to copy as much as I could, but the train started to move.

I took a deep breath and pulled out my paper. With my finger I traced the title, "Van Gogh's Eyes." Under the title Ms. Dennis had written in red ink, *Good job. You've done a lot of research, and you are very familiar with your subject. You've caught the haunting of van Gogh.* She'd given me an A.

Wow! Ms. Dennis thought it was good. I hugged the paper. I had believed it was good, and now I knew. I loved those words: *the haunting of van Gogh.*

The crow cawed, and I looked up, feeling little prickles in the nerves along my neck bones. If you got an A, people expected more of you. Being ignored was an arm's length from anyone's reach, and I was used to it. But her words made me want to try more artistically. But if I tried, what would happen? What if I wasn't really good? Would it change the way I felt about my art? Art had always been my own safe world. The world I created. I stood up and started walking. I stumbled as my foot rocked over a large stick on the ground.

I went up to the tracks again that Saturday morning after visiting Gram. The ground rumbled and the air vacuumed and filled as the Amtrak train pulled in from the east. A college-age girl got off at the station. She was plump with curly brown hair. She had on a sweatshirt that said TEMPLE UNIVERSITY. The sweatshirt reminded me of the Mona Lisa's ideas about college. I laughed. Who went to college to study art? Nobody makes a living from art. Not while they are alive, anyway. Look at van Gogh.

I picked up the sketchbook, and I got my colored pencils from my backpack. I tried to draw the sweet gum tree across the road. The way the leaves turn every color at one time—yellow, orange and purple—is special, and sweet gums are one of the last trees to turn, but the sketch wasn't working, and I threw down the sketchbook. I was more interested in the color than the tree, so I'd have to try painting it at school.

• • •

In the evening, Todd and I went bowling again. We drove into town and pulled into the dark parking lot behind my apartment. While we were still in his truck, he pulled me into his arms and kissed me and I kissed him back, and then we were lying on the seat. Both of us were breathing hard, but I wasn't afraid. This was nothing like before. This was Todd. I could trust him.

There was some laughing outside. Todd pulled away and looked out the front window. His mouth twitched a little, and I could see he was nervous. "Some kids hang around here looking for fights. This probably isn't the greatest place," he said.

"And," I said, "it's late, and you have to get up and work anyway." I nuzzled into his neck, kissed it, and sat up next to him.

When he left, I ran up the stairs to the apartment. I was soaring. It was like I'd finally caught the ultimate wind current that was going to lift me up.

I was scared because life was so good. I was living on tiptoe, moving from one thing to the next. I barely breathed, afraid that the slightest misstep, the slightest noise, could mess things up. I willed myself to believe that it could go on, but late that night, when I couldn't sleep, I heard the whistle of the train.

Ten

Wednesday night I did a load of laundry while I waited for the phone to ring. For a change, Stella was at home. She was banging around in the kitchen. She was working night shift again, so I knew she'd take off close to eleven.

The phone rang. A warm rush flowed down my arm as I reached for it. Even my arm got excited at the thought of Todd. Was I crazy about him or what? I could hear Jazz's voice say "infatuated." "You are infatuated!" *Yeah,* I thought. *So what?*

"Hello? . . . Oh hi, Todd. I was hoping it was you." I took the phone into my room. Todd told me that he was having a hard time writing his art paper.

It seemed that just being good at pottery didn't automatically mean you could write a good paper about artists or their theories. I didn't have the heart to tell him what I'd gotten on my paper, so I said, "I guess I'll see you Friday at the game. Pizza City?"

"Won't work," he answered. "There's a college scout coming to the game, and my parents want me to talk to him. They've been giving me a hard time lately. My dad keeps repeating the old *What happened to responsibility?* and *I'm neglecting my chores* stuff, and Mom says I'm not keeping up with my schoolwork. I got a C on a calculus test two days ago."

I was quiet while I let his words sink in. I could easily imagine the conversations. I pictured his parents, Vern and Irene. I stared at them at the football games every week. They sat right up under the light-blue box at the top of the stands. Todd's mom was always hunched in blankets, only her poodle-perm curls and round glasses were visible. Her glance darted around, like a sparrow in the square. Todd's dad always stood, arms folded across his broad chest. He wore a baseball cap, and the skin on his face and hands was that reddened bronze of a farmer.

I realized that while I was thinking about his parents, I'd missed what Todd was saying. "A concert? Where?" I asked.

Stella appeared in the bedroom doorway.

"Hershey Park Arena—Brooks and Dunn—this Saturday night," he repeated. I actually liked a few of their songs. I'd heard them enough in Todd's truck.

"I'd love it." I looked at the clock and realized I had to get over to Irma's house. "I have to go babysit. I'll see you tomorrow at school." We hung up.

"Is this guy getting to be a regular thing?" Stella asked.

"You could say that," I answered.

"Is he good to you?" Stella asked.

"Yeah," I answered, wondering where this was going.

"That's good. Don't take any shit from him," Stella said. *Okay,* I thought. I wondered what qualified as shit to her. She must have had some definition in her mind, but judging from her past choices, I wasn't sure what it was. Still, she was giving me some sober advice on relationships. That was unique.

"I won't," I said. I wondered about Lou. Did she think he was good? She'd been spending time with him, and he seemed nice enough, polite even. Of course I'd only seen her with him a couple of times on the way to or from places, but the cat thing had sounded good. You could put up with wifebeater T-shirts. "I've got to get going. I'm babysitting Tommy."

I liked babysitting Tommy. As soon as Irma left,

the apartment was my house, and Tommy was my baby. It was my own little world. But the one I was going to have after I married Todd would be better. He'd give me a beautiful house by the creek and lots of children. I would have a bright-yellow room for painting, which I would do in my spare time. And we would never move. At all.

I was good with Tommy, and he wasn't even my own baby. I pictured myself as the world's greatest mother. Actually, Tommy was pretty easy to take care of because he was a happy baby. Strange, because his mother was so unhappy. The woman hadn't smiled at me yet. I picked up Tommy and said, "Shows you not everything is genetic, thank God."

I fed Tommy, bathed him, and washed his hair. He splashed away. When he was dry, I sprinkled a lot of baby powder on him, because I loved the smell. I held him on my shoulder and walked up and down in the little apartment singing him songs from *Sesame Street* until he fell asleep. After I settled him in his crib, I sat on the couch, pulled my sketchbook out of my backpack, and drew lots of pictures of him. Van Gogh liked babies too.

That night as I lay in bed, curled around Spider-Man, I could feel the mind-ache. It was worming deeper, slowly invading. Why couldn't I just trust the good in my life? I mean, Todd had called, and we were going to a concert, weren't we?

What was the word that Vincent had used? He had been feeling okay, but he still felt a vague unhappiness. No, the word was *undercurrent*. An undercurrent of sadness.

Undercurrent was such a good word. One of my first memories was in Malibu when I was three and the undercurrent had grabbed my legs and pulled me out into the ocean. My hands grabbed at the sand and caught nothing, but my mouth was full of salt. After that, water fear lived in my legs, turning them shaky for years. I was ten years old before I learned to swim. But now the undercurrent was everywhere. I could feel it pulling my feet, leaving my hands holding on to nothing. I wished by the stars that glowed on my ceiling that the mind-ache would be gone forever.

In the truck on the way to the concert, Todd asked, "How's your grandmother doing?"

"About the same, but I still enjoy being with her." I was glad that he had asked.

"On my way to pick you up, I drove by my grandmother's place. She was out working in the garden, getting it ready for winter. Being hardworking is a big thing in my family. She'll probably live and work until she's ninety-five. My great-grandmother did."

I realized I didn't even know how old my grandmother was.

The concert was perfect: the music was sadder and sweeter than I thought it was going to be, and it saturated the air. It pushed and pulled the crowd to stand, sway, and clap. We gave in and stood up on the next-to-last song, and I leaned back into Todd and he put his hand on my thigh. A shudder went from my head to my toes. During the last song, the heat between us intensified. Todd was pressing into my back, and then he bent down and lifted my hair off my neck, winding it around his hand. He kissed my neck and then my ear and whispered that he wanted me.

We left the concert before the last song ended, and Todd headed for the back roads so fast it made my stomach lurch. My head was spinning. In ten minutes we were parked on a road with no one else around, and we ran to the back of his pickup. I was in Todd's arms and I was sober, fully alive, and feeling everything from my fingertips to my toes. Todd kept repeating that he wanted me as we lay down on an old quilt. I told him repeatedly that I loved him. I felt safe under him. I was sure that my fourteenth birthday was leaving my body. It seemed like forever ago.

Afterward I lay there curled against his body under an old brown blanket and stared at the stars above me. I didn't want to forget the refuge of that moment. I wanted more of it.

Sunday, Monday, Tuesday. Todd hadn't called. Usually he would have, by then. *At least I'll see him in art class,* I thought as I headed to school Wednesday morning. But in class, he smiled and looked away. Sometimes he stared at his hands, and sometimes he stared out the window. I couldn't decide if he was remembering something good or unsure what to say after something so important. He'd had few girlfriends, being shy, and maybe he didn't know what to do next. I put it down to his lack of experience. I wanted to know what was going on with him, but I didn't want to seem pushy.

After school, I saw Gram, then went home and found that Stella was there. She was in the bathroom pulling on the skin at the corner of her left eye. "What are you doing?" I asked.

She turned from the sink and looked at me. "I'm thinking there has got to be something I can do about these wrinkles, but, Hell's bells, I can't figure out what, short of using Scotch tape to pull them up." She shook some foundation on her fingertip and rubbed it into the wrinkle. She turned around to look at me and tapped on her plastic watch with her fingernail. The half-peeled-off orange fingernail polish made quite a contrast with the pink watch face.

"Why aren't you at the diner?" I asked. She'd been eating at the Capstone Diner with Lou when he was in town. Lou was a regular at the Capstone according to Stella, and that hadn't changed after he'd met her.

I don't know where they went out for drinks. It was surprising, but I didn't even know what Stella's favorite bar was in this town. Usually I knew that before I knew much else. It was the first place we headed for whenever we moved. She usually settled on one bar in her quest to find a man.

Stella thought I was old enough to be "on my own" by ten, which was fine by me. She always left me a note with the name of the bar. Sometimes I'd gone looking for her. At times, I needed money for school, or even food.

I hadn't gone to any bars to find her in this town. I was too old for that. We had communicated so little in the last two months, and I'd had no need to find her. I was essentially on my own; the only thing I didn't do was pay the bills.

"Lou's on a long trip," Stella said. "Cross-country, I think. He won't be back till next week."

"Not his usual route, I guess." What else was there to say? *How are his cats?*

"Nope, but when he gets back, he's taking me to his place up along the Susquanita. I'd like to see it. See where he's from." She walked out to the kitchen sink. I sat down in the cracked brown Naugahyde recliner.

What did she mean? Sharp little breaths and dizziness hit me at the same time. I'm like a dog when it comes to a change in the wind. My instincts howl before the faintest touch of breeze ruffles my fur. I hadn't paid much attention to Stella lately, and she'd caught all but my dog instincts by surprise.

"See it?" I said. Since when did Stella take pleasure trips with men to see their houses?

"Oh," Stella said. "Merritt sounds like a nice town, so I thought I'd check it out. You know, see what-all is there." She wouldn't look at me. She was pulling on the yellow plastic gloves like she was going to do dishes. *See what-all is there? Why?*

I'm not listening to any more, I thought, mentally putting my fingers in my ears and humming la-la-las in my head. "Did Todd call?" I asked.

"Nope. Hey, I still haven't met this mystery man. Maybe I should."

"Maybe," I said. I wasn't volunteering information. I watched Stella dashing around before she left and decided she probably wouldn't follow through with whatever this Lou thing was. Planning wasn't her style; she was more spur of the moment, so I didn't need to get too uptight.

I tried to watch television, but without cable we only got one station, so I picked up *Cat's Cradle* by Kurt Vonnegut. It was a book John Mark had given me, but I just couldn't get into it.

Call me, Todd. Call me, Todd. I sent the thoughts out across the night, willing the telepathy to work. It had worked at his football games. He hadn't gotten hurt. My mind went back to us in the truck over and over, picturing each detail, feeling each detail.

I got up and paced, and then stopped to look out the window at the stars. They were bright. I focused on them, willing the bleakness away. The word *sadness* just didn't touch the isolation in my head. It pushed on my shoulders. This steel-edged blue was made up of same-old, same-old, but it was tinged with the slightest bit of panic.

The phone rang. I willed myself to be calm, walking to get it, but my neck was so tense, I had to keep cracking it to try to loosen it up. It didn't work.

It was Todd. "I'm sorry I didn't call earlier. I had tests this week and it's busy here and I'm trying to keep my parents off my case."

My neck relaxed. "Thanks for Saturday night," I said.

"Yeah," Todd said. "Saturday night. I had a good

time. I mean the concert was great, and you are great. And I think I'm saying *great* too many times."

It sounded fine to me. I wasn't complaining. "Thanks," I said. "For everything, I mean." I paused, unsure of where to go on from there. I was picturing his body, his eyes. What was I supposed to say?

Todd wasn't saying anything either. I supposed he was feeling as awkward as I was about just shifting into everyday topics.

When the silence had gone on for way too long, I said, "I guess I'll see you at Pizza City on Friday night."

"Can't. Sorry. There's a party for the football team after the game. It's here at our house." I wondered if the cheerleaders were invited. Their peppy humanoid alien faces filled my mind. Maybe their bloodless reptile friends had been invited too. I was angry, and all of a sudden I was fighting tears and had to pull the telephone from my mouth to cover it with my hand. Why was I crying? God, it was pathetic. The slightest thing made me paranoid.

Finally he said, "Maybe we could go bowling Saturday night, a couple of games."

I couldn't talk. I grabbed some tissues and wiped my nose, which was dripping by then.

"Jude?" he said.

"Okay" was all I could get out.

• • •

The next day as I walked home after school, there was a definite chill in the air. I walked by a house with a fence made of gray stone. The top of the fence had white stones sticking up instead of lying flat like the other stones. Their jagged points were sharp eyeteeth waiting to get anyone who leaped over. The apple tree had gnarled lifeless branches. I glanced up at the house. It was close and small, and the windows were tightly shuttered. Who would want to jump the fence?

The mind-ache had been getting worse all day. I pushed my knuckles into my temples. It rarely helped, but nothing else did either. I'd been planning to go straight to the Care Home, but I needed to focus first.

I went to the spot on the tracks by the signal light. I bent down and felt the tracks. No train yet. I heard the far-off sound of the whistle as it slowed a bit and came into the other side of Ellenville. It would pick up speed again by the time it got out to where I was. I climbed up to the rock ledge, so that I could see it awhile before it got to me. I stared at the lights. I stared, but I couldn't focus on van Gogh's eyes. The train went by and I sat there, but I couldn't keep my mind still.

Even though Todd and I were still going out on Saturday, I felt a specific squiggle of fear. For some reason I just couldn't push it aside. Probably just the past junk in my life affecting me, I told myself. But

Todd had waited a couple of days to call after making love, which was something so important to me, to us, to our relationship.

What if he didn't love me? He loved me, I told myself. In the next instant, I realized he'd never actually said it.

"Get ahold of yourself," I said. I was talking out loud to myself. That was scary. I zipped up my jacket.

I walked. I heard the crow, the turf crow. Another joined him. They screeched at each other. I looked and saw that a whole bunch were in the trees across the tracks, screeching and screeching at one another.

What if nothing was different here? But things were different; there was Gram and Todd. Would I ever have a home, a story? Somehow Gram was my story even if I still didn't know what that was. She was my family, and Todd was my home in the future. Wasn't he?

The pressure in my head increased. Damn crows. I found a rock and threw it at them. I stood up and threw more rocks, screaming, "Shut up! Shut up!"

The crows flapped up, circled, and then landed right back in the same place. Exhausted, I sat back down on the rock. Other people had sadness, swirling thoughts, questions, didn't they? **Maybe it would be better if you weren't here.**

I jumped up and shook my head. I wrapped my

long black scarf around my neck and stuck my hands deep in the pockets of my favorite jeans. Not my good jeans; my favorites are ripped in each knee. Then I walked back into town to the Care Home. I tried to stare at the windows of the row houses along the way. I wanted to see my eyes, but I couldn't see myself. The row houses stared back blankly.

When I got to the Care Home, I went right to the sink and stared at my eyes. What would they say? They were my eyes, but they looked like van Gogh's too. I wasn't sure of the color. Sort of brown. A rising creek tumbling around rocks, clouded with silt.

I turned to Gram. At least she was still the same. Nothing had changed here. "How are you?" I asked her.

Same as always, but what about you? You look worried.

"I am. I really love Todd. I want things to go right. I couldn't handle it if I thought he didn't want to be with me."

Don't sabotage yourself, Jude. It isn't as bad as you think. I know it. You are lovable, Todd or not. Remember that.

Could that be true? I wondered. God knew I wanted to believe it, but nothing in my life had said that so far. I started straightening, watering, and cleaning. I hummed, but it came out all tuneless. I could see these flat two-dimensional notes hanging in the air, each dangling from its own tail. My voice got quavery. I squeezed Gram's hand.

"I love you. Take care."

I love you too, and don't forget: I will always be here for you.

Eleven

While Jazz, John Mark, and I were eating lunch on Friday, Jazz said, "So how's Todd?"

I looked at John Mark. He picked up his peanut butter sandwich and started eating. There was something white in the sandwich.

Jazz put her sandwich down and stared at me. If I didn't answer, I wouldn't get any peace.

"What kind of sandwich is that, John Mark? Todd's fine."

"The sandwich?" John Mark asked. "It's honey on both slices of bread spread thickly so that it sinks in and gets good and crusty, followed by peanut butter on the one slice and cream cheese on the other. I admit—it's my own creation."

Jazz was still staring at me. She said in a quiet voice, "Explain more, please."

"Well, we had a good time Saturday night at the concert at Hershey Park."

John Mark raised his eyebrows, dropped his sandwich, and slapped both hands on the table. "Don't tell me you went to see Brooks and Dunn?"

John Mark's tastes in music were "eclectic." Anything from the Doors to Rusted Root to Bob Marley to Louis Armstrong. Anything but pop country, and he knew I listened to the Beatles.

"I'm diversifying," I said. "Allowing my tastes to expand." John Mark made a sound close to a snort, so I raised my voice and went on: "We had a good time." I twirled my straw in my milk carton and kept my eyes down.

Jazz said, "I'm working tonight. Are you going to the game, Jude?"

"No, there's a team party afterward. I'm going to skip the game."

"Then this is your lucky night," John Mark said. "I'm not working at McDonald's. I'll pick you up at the Care Home at four o'clock. I have another cemetery to show you, and then we'll go to my house. I was going to invite Jazz over to watch the entire *Star Wars* trilogy. I have the classic edition, you know, but since Jazz is working and you aren't going to the football game, you're the lucky one, Jude. We'll see who knows more lines, you or me. Jazz can come when she gets off work."

"Sounds better than freezing all night at a football game," I said.

John Mark picked me up outside the Care Home. "I'm taking you to an interesting cemetery."

"What's with you and Jazz and cemeteries?" I asked.

"Well, for one thing, they're quiet, and for another, this particular cemetery is famous around here. It holds the remains of a werewolf."

I laughed. "Thanks. I needed something to cheer me up."

"I'm not kidding," John Mark said. "That's what everyone says. It is a little plot raised about four feet above ground. That's unusual. Abnormal even."

"I'll believe it when I see it," I said, and laid my head against the cracked vinyl headrest of the car seat. He had an oldies station on the radio. We listened to a Tracy Chapman song called "Fast Car." It was about a girl who thought some guy in a fast car was going to get her out of her life as a grocery store checker. I put the word *truck* in for *car*.

We drove to a little back road not far from the Susquanita River. All I could see was a bunch of trees covered with old vines and lots of brambles and dried weeds. But on the other side of a big clump of leafless bushes, there was a stone wall surrounding a little graveyard. We got out and walked toward it. The air was brittle, but not cold. It was at attention.

"I love this little sign on the front of the fence," I said. " 'Within this God's acre rest the descendants of Hans Groff.' Doesn't sound like werewolf stuff to me." When I looked over the wall, I saw that the earth was built up. I pulled myself up on the wall and started sketching.

"A clever trick," John Mark said. "Don't be fooled. It's a werewolf. Why else would the cemetery be out here all by itself, not close to a church?"

" 'Together in life, together in death,' " I read from Hans Groff and his wife's stone. "Maybe Hans thought he could rest if he knew that his family was going to be close to him, and they were all nonchurchgoers. Maybe he committed suicide and they wouldn't bury him in consecrated ground."

"Nope, it's a werewolf. People have seen him," John Mark said.

"Don't tell me. Only at full moon, and only during the seventh month," I said.

"No, really. Weird stuff has happened here. A bunch of kids came out here and took pictures at twilight, and there was a swatch of light across a stone. It was like pure energy. I saw it. They even took it back to the developer to see if the flash had done it or if anything was developed wrong, but there wasn't."

"Well, light isn't werewolves. I love it here. It's so sad and private. I wonder if someone could still get buried in here."

"I don't know," John Mark said.

I jumped into the cemetery. An old Pepsi can and a blue plastic cup were sitting on Hans's grave. I picked them up, patted the ground, and climbed back up on the wall. "There now, I feel better. I think it will be my private mission to see that this cemetery is cared for. Rest in peace, Hans."

"I told you it was interesting," John Mark said as we walked to the car.

"Interesting yes, lonely maybe, but inhabited by werewolves, no," I said. "It's peaceful. What can I say? I like cemeteries too. I'm glad that Hans had his own little acre in the end."

"Yeah, I agree with you. Thanks for bringing the trash into Mom's car; she'll appreciate it," he said as I put the can and cup in the backseat.

"Anytime," I said.

"Let's go get a pizza," John Mark said.

We got some pizzas and then drove to John Mark's house. It was large and tan with forest-green trim. We settled into an overstuffed green couch in the family room and put the pizzas on the coffee table. His house, his life, seemed so normal.

"How come you know so much about small when you don't seem to live there yourself?" I asked.

"I used to live there. From first grade on, I couldn't seem to get anything right, and I got bored easily," John Mark answered. "I got into trouble, and most of the time I never knew why. They said I had 'learning disabilities.'" He held his hands up and made quotation marks.

"Anyway, I got small. It made sense. Nothing I ever did was good enough for my teachers anyway, and I seemed stupid even though inside I knew I wasn't. My IQ is close to genius." Trust him to tell the truth.

"I had a friend who was a lot like me. Always thinking up fun stuff to do. You know, crazy stuff. Made life bearable." John Mark was pulling the pepperoni off the second pizza and stacking the pieces up.

"Was it Jazz?" I said. She seemed the logical choice to me. He stopped and looked up at me.

"Nope, his name was Josh. He moved away the summer after sixth grade," John Mark said. He was looking at the pizza, only now he wasn't playing with the pepperonis. "He was my only friend. It changed everything."

"Like a movie going from color to black-and-white," I said.

"Yeah, nothing was the same anymore. I was a loner all through junior high. Got picked on by everyone. That's when I perfected the art of small. It was pure survival." John Mark's face was white. He was frowning down at his shoes. He tied and untied his black shoelaces. They had little white skulls printed all over them.

"Life sucks," I said. For a while we were quiet. I drank Diet Coke, and John Mark finished off a two-liter bottle of Mountain Dew.

He threw the bottle across the room at a trash can and went on. "The summer after eighth grade, we moved here."

I stretched my arms out in front of me, then clenched my hands and turned them palm outward and stretched again. I circled my head to the right and then to the left. I realized I'd forgotten my fears for a little while, but they hadn't forgotten me.

"It seems like you don't need to be small anymore. You do your own thing. Did the move here change that somehow?" I said. Moving had always made things worse for me.

"No." He drew the word out. "I decided I'd had enough. In E-ville I was going to be myself and to hell with it. I mean things couldn't have been worse than they were in junior high. I had nothing left to lose. And the next year Jazz came to the high school. She knew what things were like for me. She helped."

"Let's watch the movie," I said, and I settled into the couch and kneaded my neck. I flexed and un-flexed my legs until they finally began to loosen.

As the movie began, John Mark and I both said, "'A long time ago in a galaxy far, far away . . .'" I knew Princess Leia's lines a lot better than John Mark did, but he knew every line of Han Solo's, and he even made a decent Chewbacca noise.

Jazz joined us in the middle of the second movie. We actually made it through all three movies. Jazz said she would take me home. She had her mom's car.

As soon as I got in and closed the car door, the tiredness slammed into me and I yawned. Then Jazz yawned, and we kept trading yawns and laughs.

I lay in bed at home, so tired, but my mind wouldn't shut down. I kept going back to my fears about Todd even though I didn't want to. It was like running your finger over an old scar that had finally turned white. The scar doesn't hurt anymore, but it is a reminder of past pain, and the possibility of future pain.

I thought about John Mark and how he'd decided to just change things, but then, he'd had Jazz to help. Jazz was real family. I counted the stars on my ceiling over and over. I heard Stella stumble in not too long after me. Waking her up for work was going to be hard. Sometime later I fell asleep.

Saturday night, Todd picked me up and we drove to the bowling alley. He didn't say anything on the way there, but he smiled as he put his arm around my shoulder, so I put my hand on his leg. I was used to taking my cues from other people in order to figure out what to do. It didn't seem like he had any issues, so I wasn't going to push anything. The bowling alley was packed, and so smoky I could hardly see. We ended up sharing a lane with an older couple we didn't know, so we didn't talk much.

After bowling we went over to the Landon Diner, but Todd was quieter than usual. Long years with Stella had taught me to play it safe, observe, and be quiet when I wasn't sure what the other person was going to say next, so I didn't say much. I gave one- or two-word answers to his two questions about my day. I was comfortable with my own silence. I was concentrating on his. Todd ate a whole plate of fries while I ate two of mine. I doodled in catsup with another one.

Todd said, "Are you going to eat those?"

"No," I answered, pushing the plate across the table. "Help yourself."

When he finished eating, he said, "I've got to get home to do some calculus. And my family is harvesting tomorrow, so it will be a long day." I willed myself not to react. I opened my purse and looked for lip balm. While I was putting it on, the waitress came and brought the bill. Todd walked over to pay it. I watched him, glad that I hadn't let him see my eyes. He might have seen pleading in them, and I didn't want to be pathetic. I was sure my eyes would have told him that I wanted more than just bowling and small talk. I wanted to feel safe, reassured the way I had before, when I had been in his arms.

When he came back, he sat down. I was surprised that he wasn't immediately moving toward the truck. I pretended to brush food off my legs, but I was really kneading my knuckle on my thigh. Then I stacked his plate on mine and pushed our glasses toward the edge of the table.

"You want to go for a ride?" he finally asked. I almost fell sideways with relief. I hoped the ride would end up with us making love. I wanted him to slowly kiss me all over, telling me that he loved me. But when we parked, Todd just pulled me around to the back of his truck and it was over in a few minutes.

Afterward, Todd pulled the quilt around us. Then he hugged me as I shivered on the cold truck bed. I whispered to Todd that I loved him. He kissed me on my ear. We heard a car in the distance, and we stuffed ourselves into our pants as fast as we could.

He didn't say anything when he dropped me off in front of the apartment. As I went upstairs, my brain said, *See? Everything is fine,* but a little buzzer located somewhere near my stomach kept going off like a demented alarm clock. It said things weren't so fine.

As I got ready for bed, I realized that he hadn't said that he loved me. They're just three words, and God knows they're overused, but I wanted to hear them anyway. I couldn't help it.

I whispered them out loud in the dark. I could almost see them drifting up toward the stars on my ceiling. The very sounds of the words themselves could produce reality. They did for me. If Todd said them to me, they would lay claim to a part of his soul, like fence posts around a field. Of course, he could just lie and say those words to make me happy. But Todd wasn't like that; there was a deep-down honesty about him that I believed in.

When we lived in California, I slept in the laundry room. One night, a bird flew into our dryer vent and got stuck. The awful flapping of its wings as it kept beating against the vent woke me up. I wanted the bird to get out, but I didn't know how to help it. I peeked into the dryer, but it wasn't in there. I yelled for Stella, but she didn't come. The bird kept making this awful screeching noise, and when I couldn't stand it any longer, I jumped out of bed and hid in the closet. I covered my ears and hummed. An hour or so later, when I came out of the closet, I heard one noise, and then it was quiet. I screamed for my mother again and again, but I was alone with the dead bird in the vent.

Sometimes I wake up feeling like the bird is inside of me. It's beating its wings, and this god-awful screeching is going on. When the noise stops, I'm left with the dead silence. It wasn't a good sign that I woke up with the bird on Monday morning.

In poetry we were reading Ezra Pound and starting our big writing projects, writing our own poetry books. A lot of my poems had ideas from van Gogh. I read his letters at night when I couldn't sleep. My poem for Tuesday was "A Way of Looking."

Van Gogh had gone on believing and looking for the same things, even though his life just took one bad turn after another. I still loved Todd. Was that so dumb? I didn't think my love life was going to turn out like van Gogh's tragic romance. I hoped not. Look what it did to him. I could feel the frenetic cells inside my head. Were they van Gogh's or mine?

I was beginning to hate the melodrama of it all. It was becoming too Stella. Was the melodrama floating around me like the leftover smell of cooked fish in the kitchen on a winter day? Could others smell it?

John Mark said that he was getting a car sometime that week. He and his dad were going looking, and he was starting practice for *Romeo and Juliet*, even though the play wasn't until March. That translated to we wouldn't be seeing him much.

Our football team had made it to the district play-offs, so Todd rushed out of art class after ten minutes. More practice.

I tried to paint a sweet gum tree, but I couldn't get it. The colors ran together. They weren't strong enough. They muddled into gray, gray, gray.

Twelve

I read John Mark's poems during lunch on Wednesday while he ate his latest creation, sliced bananas between honey and marshmallow crème on white bread. What a sugar high! I wasn't hungry and hadn't even packed a lunch.

In art, I painted a bar. It looked somewhat like van Gogh's famous red-and-green café picture. Fierce red stained the walls inside the bar. Green lights hung over the pool table, and the gray-white faces of the people had slashes of eyes. Black and heavy like Stella's after a hard night's drinking. This picture was different from anything I'd done before. I began painting a second one. My hand had a life of its own. I just watched it.

The painting was of the art class. The walls were splashed with pale yellow light. A hand smashed a sculpture of raw red clay. I painted myself sitting in the corner of the room on Vincent's chair. I painted crows on each of my shoulders. As I painted, I could feel them pecking at my neck.

That afternoon I stayed longer than usual up at the tracks. The wind flared at me, its hackles raised as if I was trespassing on its space. I needed the focus, though, so I stayed, even though my hands were red and my face was numb when I left. I went to see Gram.

"Todd hasn't called me," I said as I swept the room.

He means a lot to you, doesn't he?

"Not a lot; he means everything. Things could be different with him. This guy could rescue me from my present, even my past. My whole life could change with him. I could actually have a future."

What if he doesn't think the same way? What if he isn't looking to change his whole life?

I put the broom into the corner and went to check the leaves on the violets. "Impossible. I know he loves me, and he needs me. It's his parents, or maybe he's under a lot of pressure with grades and football. I'm sure things will be fine."

Do you really believe that?

I couldn't answer. I gave her the "love you" squeeze.

I didn't want to go home if the phone wasn't going to ring, so I sat by Gram's bed for a whole hour, not saying anything. I wasn't down exactly; it was more like a frenzied tension in my mind. Plain old miserable would have been better than the ragged zagging that started in my head and radiated down. If only I could make it stop. I pulled my sketchbook out and drew my grandmother.

At home I got tired of sitting around waiting for the phone to ring. I screamed at it, but it didn't scream back. The place was a dump. I decided to clean. I started with the dishes and moved on to the floor, but nothing helped the faded blue linoleum with big cracks in it. I even cleaned the walls. The paint was so bad that scrubbing took it off. The bare patches looked worse.

The phone rang and I jumped to answer it, but it was only Irma asking me to come over and babysit Thursday night. I said yes. It had been a while. I was going to have to look for another job if she didn't keep calling, and I didn't want another job.

Todd wasn't in art on Thursday. Maybe he was sick, and that was why he hadn't called. I decided to call him that night after I got back from Irma's.

I was a little late when I went over to Irma's

apartment. "It's about time, honey. I'm going," she said when she opened the door. I stared directly at her mouth, but staring and hearing couldn't bring her words into my brain.

"Baby teething."

I had to listen. *Focus*, I told myself.

"He's drooling and a little fussy."

I noticed she was looking at me sort of funny. I nodded. After she left, Tommy started to cry, so I picked him up. The wind had died down, so it wasn't quite as cold outside. I bundled him up and took him for a ride in the orange-checked stroller, thinking it might distract him. When we got to the park, he watched a few squirrels that were running ahead of us, but he started fussing again. I took him out of the stroller and felt the small of his back for fever. Stella had never checked the forehead. His back did seem warmish, so I put him in the stroller and headed back toward the apartment. He whimpered all the way home.

"Please," I whispered. "Please." I jiggled him on my hip while I hunted through the bathroom cupboard for some children's pain reliever. There wasn't any. I grabbed the money Irma had left on the table to pay me. As we walked to the Turkey Hill convenience store, I kept putting the pacifier in Tommy's mouth, but he kept spitting it out. When I got back to Irma's, I gave him the children's Tylenol I'd bought, but it didn't do any good.

I couldn't think of any songs, so I turned on the TV to the local channel. Irma didn't have cable. I pulled Tommy's playpen in front of the TV and put him in it. I tried rubbing his gums, but he bit down hard on my finger with his two teeth. "Ouch!" I yelled. Then I settled back on my haunches staring through the mesh of the playpen. Tommy and I were eye to eye.

NOTHING WILL EVER CHANGE.
NOTHING WILL EVER CHANGE.

My throat stiffened inside. I choked. I ran into the bathroom to get myself some aspirin. I looked in the mirror. "Stop it. Stop it," I said, banging at my temple. I grabbed the aspirin bottle and took a couple. Tommy was crying now. He and the television were too much.

"STOP IT!" I shouted at Tommy from the door of the bathroom. I was petrified by my own screaming. I covered my mouth with my hands and sat down on the floor. I was being Stella, and I wasn't even drunk. Stupid sobs ripped me. I lay there on the floor and cried until my stomach muscles hurt too much. Tommy cried harder. The kid had the ocean in him.

I picked him up, facing him outward, but he arched his back, flinging his head into my chest. "Ouch!" I yelled as his head hit my collarbone. I put him back down in the playpen and paced across the living-room floor. My pacing released that half-dead, old dog smell from the shag carpet. I gagged.

I decided to give Tommy a bath, and he quit crying, but he was still fretting. "Come on, Tommy, please. It's been a hell of a day." He started to rub his eyes. "At last," I said. "You must be as tired as I am." He finally fell asleep in the playpen, and I fell asleep on the couch.

I woke up when Irma came in. She didn't ask how the night had gone. I told her about the money for the children's Tylenol, and she dug around in her purse and came up with a five-dollar bill and handed it to me with an angry look, like the whole bad evening had been my fault. But I hadn't made Tommy sick. I was so exhausted when I got home that I fell into bed. It was too late to call Todd.

The next day Jazz and I went outside during lunch. I sat on the cold ground. My legs got tight with cold. The sun was shining, so I tilted my face toward it and let the warmth sink in. I asked Jazz to go to the football game with me, but she was working at Pizza City that night. Todd was back in art, but he just smiled when he left for football. What did that smile mean? Something or nothing?

After school I walked to the tracks. Smoke from burning leaves filled the air as I passed an apartment complex and neared the railroad tracks. Most of the leaves were off the trees now. The sumacs were bare trunk points, like so many arrows ready to be shot in the sky. Was everything bare, or did it just look that way because that's how I felt? When a big gust of wind came down through the tracks, a swirl of brown leaves flew up from the railroad bed in a mini whirl-wind. Was my new life, my good life in E-ville, swirling away too? I wondered if I'd ever had Todd at all.

I didn't stop at the rocks; I walked up the tracks until I heard the train whistle. I waited a minute or so and then started counting one, one thousand, two, one thousand for another minute, and then I jumped off the tracks. The train came by right after that. I walked back to the train station and headed toward the Care Home.

The air inside the Care Home was worse than ever, but maybe it was the contrast between it and the leaf-burning air outside. I went into Gram's room. I crossed to her bed and kissed her cheek. It was warm, but something was different. I stared at her face for a while. It was slack. I felt this tremor in my foot, and my toes curled up in my shoe. I edged my shoe off and stomped my foot.

"How are you?" I asked. There was no answering thought. I felt dizzy. I sat down and hummed "Hey Jude" as I straightened her bed. "I'm afraid I've lost Todd. Did you ever lose someone you loved?" She didn't reply. *Careful. Go slow,* I thought. *Breathe slow.*

I checked the violets. They looked a little limp. I could feel the air from the heater blasting up at them. It smelled dusty, old. I watered the flowers. "I'm having such a hard time with things, Gram. Sometimes I feel like I can't run my own mind. I can't make things work."

I went over to the sink and looked at myself in the mirror. I looked sick. My puffy eyes were bloodshot, and the purple half-moons under them looked like eye shadow. I'd been sleeping even less than usual in the last week. My face looked shabby and pale, but not slack like Gram's. I washed it.

I went back to the bed and sat beside her for a while with my hand over hers. I was too tired to talk anymore.

Silence echoed. I heard it in Gram's room. It was louder than a horn in a tunnel. My life was tunneling into a small space between school, the tracks, and the Care Home. It had a deafening echo.

•　　•　　•

When I got to the apartment, I dropped my backpack. It was quiet. Was Stella sleeping? I wondered. Then I saw the note on the table:

I'm off with Lou. We are going to his home to look around. I'll be back Sunday or Monday. Here's five bucks in case you need it.

Okay, I'd gotten the hint about checking out his town, but I hadn't realized she'd made actual plans and was doing it. Was she going to move in with Lou? That would be new. Men usually moved in with us and when they didn't work out, we moved on.

Was this man actually inviting Stella to live with him? I gulped, feeling the pull of anger in my chest. It was sucking the oxygen out of the air. If she moved in with Lou, I wasn't going with her. Not again. No way. I needed to stay here where Todd was. Where Gram was.

I grabbed some corn chips and heated up some Cheez Whiz in the microwave, but after a few bites, I was biting cardboard. I tried to swallow, but the sharp edges wouldn't go down. I spit them out in the sink.

I got my warmest clothes on and grabbed the afghan. I walked around the square, looking at the little white lights in the trees. The GO, BEARS banners, and the blue-and-white streamers, which were tattered by now, fluttered in the wind. Sparrows were jumping around at the base of two trees. I sat on the bench and watched one fly to the same branch about ten times.

The cold made my nose run, so I kept wiping it until I'd used up all my tissues. I headed back up to the apartment to get a pocketful of new ones, and then I left for the game. I heard the drums of the marching band long before I got to the field. People were talking and laughing; the sounds blew around me like so many puffs of air.

I sat in my usual spot and looked up to see if Todd's parents were sitting on the upper bench. Of course they were. Todd's mom was hunched in her blankets as before. Todd's dad was standing, arms folded across his chest as usual. His eyes were fixed on the players. The players jumped up and down, slapping themselves and each other. I saw Todd look up at his dad, and then quickly look away. *His father's ideas, his father's wants.* I could see them streaming down toward Todd.

The game began. I sank deeper into my afghan. Todd was everywhere. He was brilliant. He would get the scholarship; I was sure of that. The woman next to me was dressed from head to toe in blue. She leaned toward me to yell, "Go, Todd!" I leaned back and hit the knees of someone behind me.

"S-s-sorry," I stammered. Who was I in this crowd? Their screams jarred. My teeth were banging against each other. I got up, went to the concession stand, and bought some hot chocolate. I blew hard on it. The steam covered my face, warming me. I drank it slowly; then I turned and left the game, bumping into people as I was jostled out the gate. I walked toward home with tiny mummy steps, my afghan wrapped around me.

The door closed behind me with a thud. I lay on the couch, shivering, wrapped in a little world of afghan, but it didn't make me feel safe. After an hour, I got up and went to the medicine cabinet. I grabbed a bottle of aspirin and took a few. Then I lay back down on the couch and turned on the TV, staring at the white lines running through the picture.

Thirteen

The phone was ringing. I was on the couch. I must have fallen asleep there. My mouth was sour from the aspirin.

The phone had rung before, I realized as I sat up. I'd thought it was part of a dream in which Stella was yelling at me to shut off the alarm. I glanced at the clock. It was ten. Sun was coming in the window, which meant it was Saturday morning. I got to the phone by the sixth ring. "Mrs. Barnes?" Who was asking for Mrs. Barnes? Everyone called her Stella.

"This is Jude Barnes," I said "Stella Barnes is my mother."

"We need to speak to her about Eleanor Porter," the voice said.

"This is Eleanor's granddaughter, Jude. Stella is not here. Why?"

"We need to speak to Stella Barnes right away," the voice said.

"Can I take a message?" I asked. It had to be the Care Home. Was something wrong with my grandmother? I felt a lurch in my stomach, which wasn't too steady anyway.

"When will she be back?" the voice asked.

"I have no idea. What is this about?"

"Thank you, Miss Barnes. Did you say your name was Jude?" the voice asked.

"Yes, yes, it is."

"Well, thank you, Jude. We'll keep calling."

I jumped up and ran into my bedroom to pull on some other clothes. Something was wrong. I knew it. I wasn't waiting around until my mother got home. Who knew when that would be? Gram needed me now.

I grabbed my Chewbacca T-shirt and ripped off my jeans. I found my green fatigues in the dryer and threw them on. I pulled on a sweatshirt of Stella's. I grabbed my coat and put it on as I headed for the Care Home.

I raced into my grandmother's room, but it wasn't my grandmother's room, because she wasn't in the bed. It had to be someone else. It had to be a woman who looked like my grandmother.

I heard the words "Oh God" come out of my mouth. The woman was ashen. Her face was slack. The skin around her neck hung in folds. Her eyes were closed. I ran around the bed. Both eyes were closed. Both hands were lying flat beside her. I touched her cheek. She was cold. "Gram?" I said.

The door opened behind me. A nurse walked in. Her skirt swished as she moved around the bed and stood beside me. She put her arm around me. "I'm so sorry. We were waiting to tell your mother."

"Sorry?" I said stupidly. "Sorry?"

"Your grandmother had another stroke and died a little while ago."

That woman wasn't my grandmother. It didn't look like her. It wasn't her. I didn't move, and finally the nurse took her arm away. She walked quietly out of the room.

I sat down in the chair in the corner, and then I wasn't there in the chair.

I was outside the window, looking in at the scene, watching a movie with a girl and a dead woman on the bed. I could see that the girl's mouth was open, but I couldn't tell if she was saying anything. It was like a silent movie, and the girl wasn't a good actress;

her face was too empty. And then the bed was empty. And suddenly I was there in the room touching my grandmother's hand, grabbing it. Somehow I needed to go back. Turn everything back.

"I'm sorry, Gram. I'm so sorry I wasn't here. I let you down. I knew something was wrong. I should have stayed. I would have."

The door opened again, and a heavyset woman with black glasses came in. I dropped Gram's hand. The woman's heels clicked on the floor. She was dressed in a green pantsuit, and her hair was black and stiff. It didn't fit her yellowy skin. "Hello. I'm Jean Shrock. I believe I spoke to you earlier." I recognized the phone voice. "It's important that I speak to your mother about arrangements."

Arrangements? What did she mean by that? "Your grandmother didn't leave any instructions with us, and since we knew that she did have some family . . . well."

Arrangements. What a stupid word. She was talking about a funeral—a freaking funeral. I punched the side of the bed. My other hand clenched as I wrapped my arm around my stomach. Stella wouldn't have planned for a funeral, and I certainly hadn't thought about it. Thinking about a funeral would have been like wishing Gram dead.

The woman was watching me. Wanting me to say something. I looked down at Gram, wanting her to tell me something, but she didn't, couldn't. Then I heard the words **not ever again** in my mind, and the anger drained out of me. As it left, the energy in my body left with it.

"Stella isn't here. I'm not sure when she'll be back," I said. The woman was quiet. A little crease formed between her eyes. "She's gone for the weekend at least, but I'm sure there were no arrangements made. Stella and my grandmother didn't get along. I guess you can talk to me."

The woman's face smoothed out. "I'm sorry. I didn't realize your mother was away for the whole weekend. Why don't I just stay here with you? We can talk about it all later."

The woman came and stood beside me with her arm on the back of the chair. I didn't know what to do. Finally, I decided to call someone. I needed a familiar voice, someone to care. I went out to the nurses' station and asked to use a phone. I looked up Todd's number in the phone book. My fingers shook and the pages kept sticking together. I found the number; there was only one Vern Rineer listed. After a few rings, Todd's mother answered in a high voice: "Hello?"

"Is Todd there?"

"No, he isn't. He went to his cousins' after milking. We're all going for a family reunion tonight. Who is this?"

"This is—" I stopped and hung up the phone. I took a few steps away from the nurses' station. I was wobbly. After a few minutes, I was a little stronger. I went back to the desk and looked up McDonald's.

"Is John Mark Miller there?" I said when the call went through.

"Yes, just a moment," someone said.

"John Mark? Please come. It's Gram. She, she . . ." I said.

"Where are you?"

"At the Care Home," I said.

"Stay there. I'll come."

About ten minutes later, John Mark came into the Care Home. He was wearing his McDonald's uniform, and his long hair looked funny under the cap. "I've got another hour or so to work. How about coming to McDonald's? I'll get you some food, and you can wait until I'm done." I nodded.

John Mark held my arm, and we started toward the door. "Where's your coat?" he said.

"In there." I nodded toward my grandmother's room; only it wasn't her room anymore. John Mark went in and came out with my coat. He handed it to me, and we walked to his car. His new old car.

I hadn't ridden in it yet. I opened the door, and it smelled like a pine tree air freshener. It smelled better than the Care Home, or the heavy grease smell that hung around the McDonald's when we got there. John Mark led me to the corner booth. I told him I wasn't hungry, but he brought me a vanilla milk shake. I sipped a little.

John Mark began mopping the floor. It wasn't long before he was finished, and we headed out the door. "Where's your mom?" he asked.

"Away. Somewhere. She's with this guy, Lou the trucker. She went to his home in Merritt, wherever that is. Said she'd be back Sunday or Monday."

"Why don't we go to my house?" John Mark said. I nodded.

When we got there, I sat on the green couch in the family room. A candle filled the room with the smell of vanilla. I heard John Mark's voice, but it was just a sound in the background.

Sometime later Jazz came in. She knelt in front of me and circled me with her arms. I stared into her hair. After a while she said, "My mom wants you come over and stay with us."

Jazz's house was warm, and as I took my jacket off, I heard her mom making noise in the kitchen. I smelled both coffee and cinnamon, and wondered if she was baking.

I lay down on the couch and tried to remember Gram's face, the different violet plants in her room, the last thing I'd actually said to her, but I couldn't pull anything up. The day was getting hazy, vague, but it was so important. I wanted to remember, see, every detail about my grandmother. Instead my mind was full of the smells in Jazz's house, the feel of the corduroy material of the couch pressing into my cheek, and the color brown: brown leaves swirling up from the tracks, the brown couch in my own house, the brown coat thrown over the chair across the room. Maybe all my thoughts had turned brown.

That night Jazz's mom took me up to her sister's room, the sister at college. As I took in the room with its details, I realized that the numb was beginning to wear off. The wallpaper was beige with blue-and-white flowers, and there was a matching border around the top. The floor was hardwood. There were blue rag rugs on it. The bed had a blue, pink, and white quilt. The patches were in the shape of a giant star. There was an old gray teddy bear in a blue sweater on top of the bed. He looked like he'd been around for a while. There were framed pictures everywhere. Two groups of girls had their arms around each other. In one picture they had on bathing suits and towels, and in another they were wearing soccer uniforms. There was a picture of a young blond frizzy-haired girl with braces, sitting on a horse. There were two different prom photos and lots of family shots.

Jazz's mom opened a dresser drawer and pulled out some sweats. She left the room, saying, "I'll bring you back a towel and washcloth."

I put the sweats on. When I pulled back the quilt, I smelled lavender. I picked up the pillow and sank my nose in it. The pillowcases were scented. Jazz's mom knocked and I told her to come in. She put a towel on a desk and said, "I hope you sleep well, Jude."

I sank down on the bed, got under the covers, and breathed in the lavender. I pulled the star quilt up to my chin and was surrounded by the safe, wrapped up in it. Then I heard the words **not ever again.** They were so loud, I thought maybe I'd spoken them. A desolation that was full and yowling stalked into my mind after the words. I hugged the bear and sobbed. I fell asleep crying.

The next morning, Jazz and I decided to drive over to the Care Home. When we went into my grandmother's room, we found the bed stripped, but the plants and picture were on the window ledge.

"I want to take her things home," I said to Jazz. "I don't want to come back here again." She went out of the room. I took the pictures off the wall. I checked the plants, and they didn't look too good. I wondered if they would make it home in the cold. After about ten minutes, Jazz came back in with a box, and we put the plants in it. She carried the box, and I took the framed picture and the drawings. Jazz had been good through what had happened with Gram, so I figured I could take her to our apartment.

As I unlocked the door, I said, "It's not the sort of place you want to hang out in." It was cold inside and I shivered. The nakedness of the apartment was such a contrast to the warmth of Jazz's house. "Not much to see," I said as she stepped in behind me.

I pressed my cold hands against my red face, wishing I could cover the embarrassment I felt when Jazz saw the sheets on the windows. "Stella broke every miniblind in the apartment. She yanks too much, and she never got around to getting anything else." We put the plants and picture on the olive-marble Formica kitchen table.

"Thanks for coming today. And tell your mom thanks for everything too." How I wished I was going back to that house!

Jazz hugged me and left. The aloneness I felt was so complete, so of a piece; there wasn't room for anything else. It was the lava moving down a volcano, engulfing everything in its way.

I took a few of Gram's plants and went into my room. I spotted my copy of *Dear Theo* on the floor. I picked it up and looked at the eyes. *God, Vincent,* I thought. *You must have felt so alone when your brother married and had a child. The one constant in your life was gone. How could you hold it together when your center was gone? No wonder you committed suicide.* Images of suicide flitted across my brain—a gunshot like van Gogh's, wrist slitting, overdosing, throwing yourself in front of a train.

I was so tired. I just wanted to sleep but was afraid I couldn't, so I took a handful of aspirin.

When I woke up, it was dark. I went into the living room. I walked over to the window and pulled down the sheet. I stared at the stars, and I heard the far-off sound of the freight train.

Fourteen

It was morning when I heard the door opening. My mother blew in. "I had a great time in Merritt with Lou. Cutest little town. I loved it up there. I even got along with his cats."

"Hi," I said as she walked toward the fridge.

She pulled the door open. "Any iced tea in here? What's with you? Are you sick or something?" She pulled out a carton of milk and poured herself a glass. She sat down at the table and began to drink. "What's this doing here?" She put the glass down so quick, some milk spilled. She had Gram's picture in her hand.

"I put it in Gram's room at the home. I was hoping that she would tell me about it, but Mom—"

She interrupted me: "*Tell* you about it? You never could leave well enough alone, Jude." I could hear the anger rising in her throat, but it didn't touch me.

"It wasn't that," I said. I thought my words sounded slow. "I needed to know something. I needed to know about myself, about you." I sat up.

"Well, *I'll* tell you about it!" she said in a clenched voice. She strode over to the couch with the picture in her hand.

"Not now," I whispered, but she went on.

"See this old man? That's my grandfather. Beat the hell out of this woman, his daughter, Eleanor, so she left home at sixteen. She married a man who died in the war. So she moved back home with her father. Why? I'll never know, except that she didn't seem to have the guts to do anything else. Only now she had a child, me. And things took up where they left off. Only pretty soon, he began beating me too. And she did nothing. *Nothing.* I think she had this cockeyed idea that we deserved it somehow. It was hell. I left and didn't look back. There, Jude. That's the story." She dropped the picture on the floor, and the glass cracked.

The phone rang. I couldn't move. Stella answered it.

"Yeah, this is Stella Barnes. Who are you?"

I figured it was the Care Home. "What? . . .

Well . . . oh." Stella was silent for a second or two. "Where is she? . . . Snyder's? . . . Okay. I'll go over today."

She hung up and turned to look at me. "Why didn't you tell me she died, Jude?" For the first time in a long while, I think she actually saw me. Jude. Her face softened, and then I felt that my face was coming apart. Morphing, melting, and I couldn't see her anymore.

I opened my mouth, but tears streamed into it. I put my hands over my face and closed my mouth. I heard Stella say, "Ah, Jude, I'm sorry. My timing is lousy, always was, but it's the god-awful truth." I felt a touch on my shoulder. I looked up. She was crying too.

We were looking into each other's eyes in spite of the tears. She turned away and said, "I guess I should go to the funeral home."

"Yes," I answered, but the word was muffled. She picked up her purse and headed for the door. She opened it, but before she went out, she turned and looked at me. She was still crying.

I didn't go to school. Stella was in a mad hurry to "take care of things." She attacked the job with the same frenzy she had when she cleaned out Gram's apartment. I stayed out of her way. I didn't feel like doing anything at home, so I wandered along the railroad tracks in spite of the wind whipping through. Irma called and I told her I wouldn't be babysitting that week. I shuddered at the thought of my last time with Tommy.

I called Jazz and thanked her for letting me stay with her, and then I told her there was going to be a service for Gram on Tuesday at the stone church close to the Care Home. I didn't want to say anything more than that. Actually I really didn't want to talk at all, so I told Jazz to let John Mark and Todd know, and I hung up. Todd hadn't called, but then I hadn't been around much on Saturday or Sunday, so maybe he had tried.

Stella and I went to the church for Gram's funeral. I hadn't been in a church before. I loved the way the sun hit the stained glass windows at an angle, which made them look illuminated from within.

I'm not sure why Stella had a service. Maybe it was her way of making something right in her own mind. There was one lily in a pot by the pulpit. I wondered who had sent it.

The minister came in and greeted Stella and me. The look behind his wire-rimmed glasses was soft. His face was creased with wrinkles, and his hand was warm as he shook mine. Jazz, her mom, John Mark, and the administrator from the Care Home came in and sat behind us. I wished that Todd had come.

I sat there with my hands in my lap, hoping that Stella would be quiet, and she was. She crossed her legs and tapped the floor with her dangling foot. She kept her eyes on the cross at the front of the church, and one hand clutched the pew seat.

The minister's voice was gentle. He didn't talk about Gram's life. I was thankful for that because he didn't know her, but then come to think of it, neither did I. He said he was reading from the Psalms. Whoever wrote the verses had experienced a lot of pain, and from the tone in the minister's voice, I knew that he had too. I stared at the colored light from the window, and the minister's words flowed around me. I was in a timeless place. Calm brushed my cheek. It settled like velvet against my skin. And then it was over. Over before I could grab it. Had it been real?

The minister stopped speaking, and Stella rushed outside to smoke, sucking in on the cigarette as if her life depended on it. I thought, *How funny—cigarettes are the last thing she should depend on for life*. The smoke stayed around her head, flattened in the moist, cold air. Stella waved at it when she saw me heading toward her with my friends. I introduced her to them.

She thanked them for coming. They left, and Stella and I walked to the Domino's behind the church. We ordered a pizza and then took it home and ate it.

My grandmother's ashes were in a container in a box on my plywood dresser. I sat on the bed and stared at my grandmother's box for a while, wondering what to do with it. I didn't know what to think of my grandmother anymore, much less her ashes. What were ashes?

Stella was working night shift, so she left. I went to bed, but I couldn't sleep. I got up and looked at the pictures in the van Gogh book that Todd had given me. There was a quote about the morning star. I wondered if I'd ever seen that star.

I stood at the window and looked for it. I saw a star that was so much bigger than the others. Had to be it. It was surveying the earth. Taking me in. I wished I could touch it.

The next day I quickly painted my first "official" portrait in art class. Once again, I was painting from some interior place. Gram's face with one eye open, one hand curling up. The background was green with blackened, curling cypress trees.

Then I painted my second portrait. It was of my

mother. She had the head of a woman and the body of a girl. She was standing next to a giant chair, twice as big as she was. It was van Gogh's chair, the one he painted after Gauguin abandoned him in Arles. Stella's dress was green with black swirls running through it. He mouth was open wide, and her eyes were blank. Her arms hung by her side, her hands empty.

My inner world was bleeding into my art. I couldn't keep things separate anymore. Ms. Dennis stopped by my desk and said, "Do you want to come by here later on today, Jude? We can talk."

"Maybe," I said. *She could handle my life,* I thought. She wouldn't be shocked by much. She might be helpful.

"How about after lunch?"

"Okay," I said, but as soon as I took up the brush and started painting, I wasn't sure I wanted to talk. It was strange, seeing my inner world on paper. It didn't feel small or safe. My isolation was a padded coat. Its layers were familiar, reassuring.

I took my mother's portrait and put it against the wall, face in. I started painting the railroad tracks. I was back in that insulated place in my painting when Todd stopped by my table, glanced down at the painting, and looked away. Then he lifted his hand and put it back down on mine. His touch pulled me to the real. I stared at his hand. He cleared his throat twice. "How about we get together Saturday?" I'll pick you up in the morning. At nine?"

At his words, relief flooded me. It was full, sweet. "Okay," I said. "Pick me up at the train station." I knew he'd be there for me. He walked away and I went back to painting.

After lunch, I didn't stop by the art room. I chickened out.

I thought that if Ms. Dennis were the least bit kind, it would do me in. I knew how to handle being ignored, or meanness even. But gentle or kind, they would get me. Like I might start crying and never stop. That's how I felt about going to see Ms. Dennis.

After school, Jazz and I went to her house. She ate some of the peanut-butter cookies that her mom had left. I made myself some coffee, grinding the beans and everything. It was good stiff Sumatra. I got high from the smell. I was on an island, surrounded by the ocean. Far away.

"Do you want to go somewhere?" Jazz asked.

"Yes," I answered. We got into her mom's car. Jazz drove us to a tiny park outside of E-ville. It was right along the Susquanita. There were a few picnic tables. It wasn't far from Hans's acre. I stood on a rock that jutted out into the river. The sun glinted on the water, and I watched it glide and swirl as the current pulled it. A leaf got caught up by the rock, circling until it got tugged away, and then I knew I couldn't hold back the flow of my life. The accumulating grief was too strong. I had to do something with it.

I decided to start by scattering Gram's ashes there. I'd let her go, along with my hopes for her. "Jazz, let's go to my house. I need to get something," I said.

We drove back, and I went in and got my grandmother's ashes and my sketchbook and a charcoal pencil.

"I'm going to scatter my grandmother's ashes there at the park," I said when I got back in the car.

At the park, I stood on the rock and said, "To you, Gram." I dumped the ashes out. "Thank you for the hope you gave me while you were here. Thanks for what we had between us. I promise it will remain untouched by anyone else's memories. I hope you make it all the way to the sea, where you can rest."

I went to the car and got my sketchbook. I sat down on the rock and sketched the river and the rock.

We got in the car, and I stared at the starry night picture on the cover of my sketchbook. Naturally, my thoughts went to van Gogh.

"Van Gogh felt that everyone left him," I said. "He felt so alone. It's no wonder he committed suicide."

"His life was so sad," Jazz said, "tragic, really."

So is mine, I thought. The exhaustion and the

mind-ache had merged and moved from a pressure to a roar that filled my brain. It was the sound of the train right as it got to me. I rested my head against the window.

That night I was up. I was glad that Stella was working nights. I stared out the window. I kept hearing Stella in my mind. She was telling me her story, narrating it to me over and over. Every time there was a space from the roar in my brain, the story was there. It loomed like the big black crows. Although it made more sense of Stella, it didn't change anything in my life. My life seemed more inevitable. The thought numbed me.

I finally saw the morning star. It wasn't until then that I realized Todd hadn't called. At that point it didn't matter; I was hollow. There was nothing left to care with. I fell asleep.

The next day was Thanksgiving. Stella slept all day because she had worked the night before, and I watched the parade on television. We didn't eat turkey.

I thought about seeing Todd on Saturday. I was glad he was around. Most hunters left for the weekend. We even had Monday off for deer hunting.

Fifteen

On Saturday morning, after another restless night, I got up. I felt queasy. Maybe I was just getting cramps. Then I realized my period was late. Two and a half weeks late, and I was usually as regular as could be. I'd forgotten about my period with all that had happened in the last couple of weeks. *Maybe it was stress,* I thought. Yeah, I'd heard about how stress affected some people. But there had been those two times with Todd. What were the chances?

I put on some clothes and went to the convenience store. I bought an early pregnancy test. I ran home and did it. When I saw that I wasn't pregnant, everything around me went white. I sat down on the toilet so I wouldn't pass out. I put my head between my legs. When I could breathe right, I sat up, alert, shocked out of my mind paralysis for the first time.

Thank God! Thank God! I thought of Stella's pregnancies. Had she been looking for something, someone, and ended up with me? I could see that, but I wasn't going to repeat her mistakes. Besides, Todd wasn't like my dad, or the first Judith's dad, or even my grandfather. I ran outside and lifted my face to the sun. It was bright on me, in me.

The wind was chilly, but I hardly felt it. I heard Todd's truck before I saw it. I knew its even hum because I'd listened for it so many times.

"Yesterday I froze my butt off working in the barn, and today it's in the fifties. Can you believe it?" Todd said as I jumped in the cab.

"Don't jinx it," I said. "God, I love the sun. 'Oh, how lovely this yellow is.'"

"Don't tell me," Todd said. "Vincent van Gogh said it."

"Yep," I said.

"Unique, Jude. You are unique. I'll give you that. Lots of people are into dead rock singers, but dead artists?" He drummed on the steering wheel to the beat of the radio's music. "I've got to tell you something. Let's go up to the rock, okay?"

"Okay," I said. "I have plenty of time."

The last time I'd been up there, the leaves had been turning. It had been the time that Todd had given me the van Gogh book. There had been swirls of crimson and gold around us and under our feet. I'd scuffed in the leaves all the way to the top. Now we crunched brown leaves underfoot as we headed to the path. The branches of the trees were almost black against the sky. It began to cloud over.

When we got to the rock, I stared out at the river. It was like I was seeing forever. The world was a big place. It was much bigger than an old apartment and a Turkey Hill convenience store. I was in a boat on the river going somewhere far away. To the ocean even. And Todd was going to take me there.

"Hey," Todd said. "Look at the bridges. Don't they look tiny compared to the river?"

"Yeah," I said. "Do you think that all rivers lead to the sea? Somebody told me that one time."

"I wouldn't know, but it sounds good. What made you think about the sea?"

"Just dreaming," I answered.

"Oh." Todd was frowning. Maybe he couldn't follow my dreaming thoughts. "I've been to Ocean City," he said.

"The sea I'm thinking about would be way beyond Ocean City," I said. "Maybe the Outer Banks or Key West or somewhere like that. Far away. Someplace where you and I could live together forever with no one to bother us."

"Why are you talking like that, Jude?" Todd said.

"It's how I feel," I said.

"Things are good," he said. "What we have right now. Hanging out, being together."

"What?" I heard my own voice get quiet. A shade away from dog mean, right before the growl.

"What we have is good. Good enough for now, Jude."

"I'm not just thinking of right now. I'm thinking of the future." My voice was rising; I couldn't stop it. "I'm an adult. I make decisions for myself. I've been on my own most of my life."

"For God's sake, we're just in high school." Todd's voice was quiet, irritatingly so.

"High school, my God!" I was almost yelling now. "In a few weeks, I'll be eighteen. Don't you get it? Of course I'm thinking beyond high school."

"Wait a minute." He stuck both hands out in front of him, palms down, and pushed them down toward the ground several times, like I was a race-car driver coming in to the pits too fast. It looked so dumb, so dense, I wanted to punch him. I dug my fingernails into my palms and bit my bottom lip. "I'm not sure I'm getting this," he said.

Where was he? Were we living on different planets?

He was everything to me. He was my dreams, my hopes. God, was I losing all that? Did he think he was going to shut all that down and give me his leftovers? How could he?

I slapped him. Hard. He stepped back; shock bleached his face, making the red handprint stand out. I was losing everything, and now him?

"Jude, I mean . . ." He stopped. It looked like he was searching for something. I hoped it was the right words. I waited, giving him one last chance to find them. "Come on. You're fun, and pretty and real smart, and I can be myself with you, but I'm going to college in the fall." I turned and began walking down the hill. "I told you that the very first time we went out. I'm playing football. You know that."

I started running. I heard him yelling my name. Fun? I'm fun? Oh and don't forget smart. Real smart too. And he could be himself with me? How stunningly nice for him.

Similar thoughts crammed my brain as I ran all the way down the hill. I yanked on the door of the truck, but it was locked. I beat on the window with my fist and kicked the tire. "Open the damn door!" I yelled when I heard Todd step behind me. He was breathing hard.

"Look, Jude." He tried to touch my arm, but I

jerked away from him. "I've been trying to find the right time to say this," he went on. "I have to concentrate on school and sports. That will pay my way through college. It's what my parents expect, and it's what I want. I don't have a choice. We can still hang around."

"Shut up!" I yelled. "You don't have a choice? What are *my* choices? I could run away like I did at fifteen, which I might end up doing anyway. Or how's this? I could stay in our apartment and work at Turkey Hill to pay the rent." I paused long enough to catch my breath. "I want to go home. Drive me home."

Todd stared at me with his mouth all hung open. How could I ever have thought he was cute? Or talented? Or anything? Whoever said love is blind knew what they were talking about.

He unlocked the door, and I jumped in. I stayed at the edge of the seat, rolled down the window, and stuck my head out. "Take me home!" I yelled.

A man in a black-and-red plaid shirt with a walking stick in his hand was at the beginning of the path. He turned to look our way. "Hey," he called, "you need help?"

"God, Jude," Todd said, and he turned the truck on and spun backward, nearly wrenching my head off.

I rubbed my neck and stared out my open window

until we were a block from my house. I was white-knuckling it as Todd drove as fast as he could, passing every car with a honk, a swerve, and the finger. That surprised me. I didn't think he had it in him.

"Let me out here. In the square. And don't bother," I said as I got out, leaving the door wide open.

"What?" Todd yelled at my back.

I yelled, "Hell, don't bother anything. Ever. I don't want to see your ugly face again. But you won't forget about me, Todd. You'll remember." I turned around and walked off.

It was a great exit, but great exits don't mean much, do they? Not when you'd rather have stayed. And that line about his ugly face? That was Stella's. I'd heard it before.

Todd swore as he leaned across the seat to close the door. Then he revved the truck so hard and fast he left black marks on the road beside me. I managed to not look until after he was gone. When I got to our building, I kicked the stair railing with my black Doc Marten boot. The rail split and part of it cracked off.

"Oh God." I ran around the apartment, ripping down all the sheets. I needed light. Lots of it. I opened the windows. I was glad Stella was working. It was only eleven o'clock. She'd be working for a while. I opened the fridge and found a little jug of low-fat chocolate milk. That reminded me of the time Lou had "stayed for breakfast."

Then it came back to me. I remembered what Stella was saying when she came in the door on the day my grandmother died. She had enjoyed her time with Lou. That probably meant she was planning to move in with him. The phone rang, and I unplugged it. I didn't want to talk to anyone. I had to get out. The pain arched in my brain.

I walked to the railroad tracks, and then I walked on them. Right down the middle of the tracks. Was I just like my mother? I slumped to the tracks. How could I have made such a bad choice? How could I have been so dumb? I suppose it was because I thought I was getting family, roots. Would I spend the next twenty years bringing home a string of men with different faces but the same kind of minds and actions? I was just like my mother. I puked my guts up right there on the tracks.

I staggered upright and kept walking. I must have walked a couple of miles, because when I finally stopped and looked at my watch, it was one thirty. I realized I had no idea where I was.

Talk about a mind bender! I was in some sort of shock zone. I once saw a picture of a train wreck. It was in a book of photographs about India. Train cars were piled up on top of one another like toy blocks a kid had knocked over. People were standing around the train. Smoke was billowing up, pouring out of the cars. There were body pieces and goats and God knows what else in a pile. The photo was black-and-white. Two people, an old man and a girl, were in the foreground. They had this blank look in their eyes. They weren't seeing the trains or the cameraman. They weren't seeing anything. They were beyond grief.

Me too. I was somewhere beyond grief. Nothing mattered.

It took me two and a half hours to get home. I watched one foot step in front of the other. My feet seemed to have more memory than my brain. I fell into bed.

"Damn it, Jude. Where is my black boot? I've got to find it or I'm going to be late for work." I sat up and looked at the clock beside my bed. It said six thirty. Had I slept through the afternoon? Since Stella was back on days and yelling about work, it was morning. I'd slept for a good fourteen hours. The door slammed.

I wandered into the kitchen and found some saltine crackers stuffed away in a cupboard. The top two crackers were stale, so I threw them in the sink. I stared at them and realized I wasn't hungry anyway.

It's morning, I thought. I should be doing

something, but I couldn't figure out what. It was hard to think. I was so thickheaded I didn't want to think. I stood in the shower and let the hot water hit my neck until the steam filled the bathroom and the hot water started running out. I toweled off, got dressed, and fell on the bed. Spider-Man jumped right on top of me. He was licking my ear, with that "Get up and do something, you lazy thing" lick.

"Poor ol' Spider-Man," I said. "I guess I haven't given you the attention you deserve. I've been talking to other people, and once again I've found them to be less than a cat. Will you forgive me, my dear friend?" I picked up Spider-Man and walked into the kitchen. I could hear his motor going.

The phone rang, and I answered it. It was Irma wanting me to take care of Tommy. I said no and hung up. I lay on the couch and thought about the last time I'd babysat him, when he was sick. Pacing with a crying baby across dog-smelling shag carpets in a dumpy apartment with no money, all alone. Was that what it had been like for my mom? I wouldn't do that to a kid.

After an hour or so, I walked back into the bedroom and lay on the bed. I stared up at the poster of van Gogh's starry night, and then at the two copies I'd made of his self-portraits, the one with the straw hat and the one without the ear.

I knew that this aloneness, my aloneness, was how van Gogh felt. I wondered if Vincent had thought that nothing could change. I *knew* nothing would ever change. I had only been fooling myself before. Gram hadn't changed anything, Stella hadn't changed, and I was just like them. My life, with its ongoing series of damn bad choices was inevitable, and I couldn't keep the pain inside anymore. The future wasn't just hanging in front of me somewhere. It was coming toward me on the tracks; its rhythm was sure and mechanical. **Maybe it would be better if you weren't here.**

I don't know how long I lay there. He watched me, Vincent did. Those insecure eyes. Those mirror eyes. He knew I couldn't escape into some imaginary art world anymore. It hadn't worked for him. I pictured the crows hovering, massing, in his last painting. He knew what I should do. I was sure of it. He would tell me.

I picked up my sketchbook and read some of the quotes. I got up and looked at the calendar by the sink. I wrote down the date, but I couldn't sketch. I flipped the sketchbook over and read the quote I'd written on the back, just below a sketch of a little star. "We take death to reach a star." Over and over it played in my mind, a scratched CD repeating the same thing. My hands started shaking, and a nerve in my neck jumped. I was breathing so hard, it was almost a pant. It wore me out and I lay down again.

I pictured the man and the girl, the glazy-eyed people in front of the train in the India photograph, and decided they were in despair, a wrecked and bottomless place. They were too tired to move after the train wreck.

I couldn't fight despair—the place or the pain. Maybe the two were the same thing. Who knew, and what difference did it make what name you called it? I was too tired. I slipped somewhere below the despair.

I stayed there for at least two days. I didn't sketch. I stopped marking time. Why get out of bed? I just wanted to sleep. I didn't go to school, and I don't remember much of anything else. Stella came in once. I told her I had the flu, and she ran out of the room. I knew that things had constricted inside me. The tunnel of my life had become a narrow interior space, and even if I crawled forever, there was no way out.

One night on my way to the bathroom I stopped and stared out the window. It was frosty, clear. It was the darkest hour; when the morning star is the brightest. Sharp clarity tingled in my scalp and went all the way down through me. My brain was as clean as the window, and I could see. A strong calm filled me, and the sluggishness left. Vincent was right. We take death to reach a star. I could do what he did. Suicide could be my way of escape.

When I got back to my room, I touched a star on Vincent's starry night picture. I had things to do. I had things to give away.

I went into the bathroom and swallowed a handful of aspirin, and then I made a list.

The next morning, I got up and went to school. At lunch John Mark said, "Good of you to join us today. I thought you were going to miss the whole week."

Jazz said, "You must have been really sick. You look awful."

"Thanks," I said. "Horrible flu."

While I was at my locker, Ms. Dennis walked up and said, "Here are the financial aid papers and some stuff from an art college in Lancaster." She handed me a manila envelope.

"Thanks," I said.

"There's a reference form in there. I'd be happy to fill it out for you. Drop it by my office sometime."

I pulled the reference form and its envelope out of the packet. I put the note that I'd written to Ms. Dennis inside the envelope. It said *Thanks for everything. The paintings are yours.* I thought she'd want them.

On the way out of poetry class, I gave John Mark my paper on van Gogh. "You didn't get a chance to read it," I said.

He took it. "I'd like to."

"I got an A on it."

"That's because Ms. Dennis likes you," he said.

"Not so," I said. "You haven't read the paper. Maybe it's that good."

After art, I put the reference envelope on a pile of papers that was sitting on Ms. Dennis's desk. I was glad that art was the last class of the day.

I went out to the parking lot and looked for Todd's truck. He was at football practice. I found the truck, and it was unlocked. I put the book of van Gogh paintings he'd bought me on the front seat.

As I walked away from his truck, I mentally checked off each item on my list. Dropping things off was moving me forward. Soon there would be nothing left.

I walked to the hobby store downtown and asked them for a box. I walked as slowly as I could in the cold. I wanted to take lots of time.

When I got home, I punched holes in the sides of the box, then I painted it a deep blue. I painted stars all over it.

I cleaned my room and put the sheets back up over the windows. I changed the litter box and put it in the bottom of the blue box. Then I put a piece of cardboard on top of the litter box. I covered the cardboard with my afghan. Then I picked up Spider-Man and put him in the box. I closed the flaps, and taped them shut even though it made me feel lousy. I picked up the box and *Dear Theo* and walked toward Jazz's house. I could hear Spider-Man clawing away inside. I held tight.

"I'm sorry, Spider-Man," I whispered. "It's not your fault. You've been the best friend ever. But Jazz will be good to you, and you'll never have to move again." Tears were coming down my face, but I couldn't wipe them away. After I made sure that no one was around, I walked to the back of the house and put the box on the porch. Their garage was behind their house, so I knew someone would see it before too long. I left *Dear Theo* there too.

I pulled a tissue out of my pocket and mopped my face and blew my nose. I went back home to get the stuff for John Mark. I walked to his house. I put my sketchbook in a big envelope. I walked to the back porch and left it between the porch door and storm door. Judging by the looks of the storm door, it might be a while before someone found it.

I went back home and scrubbed the place up. Finally, I walked up to the railroad tracks. It was only ten thirty. I had time before the freight train came. I climbed up the rock to the ledge. I put the bottle of vodka there, the one that my mom kept stashed under the sink behind the Drano. I would pick it up on my way down. I figured the combination of a bottle of aspirin and a bottle of vodka would be enough to render me good and out of it. I'd fall asleep—that was a nice way to put it—on the tracks. I'd be unconscious when the train hit me. The engineer wouldn't see me because of the curve in the tracks.

After putting the bottle down, I went higher. This time I was going all the way to the top.

I looked up at the stars. I stared and stared. It was the clearest night, and I couldn't take my eyes off those stars. As I stared, the sky seemed to get bigger and each star glowed in its place, sending light down around me. I wasn't on the hill anymore. I was in pure reality, where space, matter, and time all intersected. It was the timeless reality I had painted in the yellow picture and felt in the church. And this reality was full. I wasn't alone anymore.

I had no idea how long I was there.

There was a noise, the train's whistle. I looked and saw the lights coming down the tracks. They weren't van Gogh's eyes; they were just train lights. I didn't need to blank anything out anymore.

I wanted to live. How had Jazz said it in the cemetery? *There's got to be more than what I know so far, and*

I mean to find it! Now I knew there was more, and I was going to find out what it meant. I stepped forward to throw the aspirin bottle, but my foot slipped, my ankle turned horribly, and I fell. I hit my head and then I was sliding. Rolling.

Sixteen

When I opened my eyes, the light hurt, so I shut them up tight. I was so thirsty. I asked for water, but it sounded like *Arrrggh*. What was wrong with my voice?

Someone said, "Hey, you're stirring. I'll ring for the nurse."

A cool hand turned my face to the side. A straw slipped between my teeth. "Here, take a sip." I took one, but the water dribbled down my face. The next time I tilted my head back a little.

When I opened my mouth, "Ta" came out.

I opened my eyes again and saw a blocky form, but I couldn't keep my eyes open. I tried again, pretending that toothpicks were holding them open. A woman came into focus. She was small. Her face was round and wrinkled. She had puffy bags under her eyes. Her waves of short white hair were combed back from her face. She had on a uniform of some kind.

"I'm Helen, and it's nice to meet you," she said. "I work day shift." She winked. "And while you were sleeping away, I was just catching up on the soaps in here."

The light seemed to increase the pain in my head. I gave up and closed my eyes. Sleep drifted in.

Stabs of pain shot through my ankle, and up my leg to my knee. My whole right side throbbed. This time I opened my eyes and looked down toward the pain even though the motion sent jolts into my brain. My ankle had a cast on it that came up to my knee.

The woman, Helen, was in the room again. I put it together, the outfit, the manner—she was a nurse's aide. I pointed to my ankle.

She said, "It's broken. There are pins in there some-where, and I think you messed up some tendons."

I pointed to the side that throbbed.

"I guess you want the whole story, huh? You also cracked some ribs, and you suffered a head injury, swelling around the brain. You were in a coma for a while. When I saw you stirring, I rang for the nurse. You look more awake than yesterday."

The pain in my ankle made sense, but I couldn't put her other words together: *ribs, coma.* I couldn't remember much before yesterday. I wanted to shake my head, but that would have caused more sharp tingles. A nurse came in and said, "Are you in pain?"

"Ya," I croaked, thinking that was the dumbest question I'd heard in a long time. The nurse left the room and came back with several pills in a cup and some water. She helped me take them.

After resting a moment, I tried my voice again. "Whaa?"

"You had an accident," the nurse said. Drowsiness was getting me. Must have been the drugs. I tried for one more word, but my head turned sideways and my eyes closed.

Then Helen was there again, straightening the bed, checking on me. The blinds were open and sunlight fell across my bed. "Did you say I was here for a while?" I had a voice! It was rusty and soft, but it came out okay.

"Yes, you were in a coma for almost two weeks, but you've been in and out for the last two days."

"I don't remember what happened."

A nurse had come in and was checking my IV line. She said, "That isn't unusual. Most coma patients don't remember what happened at the time of the event." She left the room.

"What happened?" I asked Helen.

"Some kids, a boy and a girl, found you by the railroad tracks. Looked like you'd fallen from some rocks."

Yeah, the rocks, the stars, the train. I stared out the window. The whole window shifted, and I was remembering. Faces appeared there: Jazz, John Mark, Ms. Dennis, and even Spider-Man. But why was I by the tracks?

I shook my head to clear it, but that caused pain. A nurse came in and gave me a pill. I drifted off again.

I was awake, but groggy. I heard Stella's voice. My weighted eyes couldn't move, so I didn't try to open them. I let the words whirl around the room, bouncing off objects.

"Are you hearing me? God, I hope they're right, and you're coming out of the coma. I feel like I'm talking to the walls in here."

Hi, Stella, I thought. *Some things don't seem to change.* The thought brought a sigh inside, but nothing more. I heard Jazz's voice saying something about change. We'd been at a graveyard, but the words weren't quite there.

"What a nightmare!" She paused for a breath and then sighed.

I heard her steps. *Click, click, click.* "Get better, hon. Gotta go." The door opened and closed.

A man came in. His mouth opened and opened. It was cavernous. I drifted off. I woke up and Helen was there. From the position of the sunlight, I could tell it was the next day. It wasn't on my bed. It hit the wall higher up. "Was my mother here yesterday? A woman with blond-streaked hair?" I asked.

"Yes," Helen said. "She was, but she's come by here other times too. Sometimes she's come in and talked to you, but once or twice she poked her head in and said something about not finding anyone to work for her, and then she left. I guess I was supposed to pass the message on, so now you have it."

"That does sound like Stella. And the man yesterday?"

"That was the doctor. You had three other visitors that I know of, one girl and two boys." I looked out the window, tensing my shoulders as I waited for the pain in my head, and then when it didn't happen, I relaxed. Just plain old dull headache. That had to be good.

"One of the boys and the girl have come at least once a week. They introduced themselves to me as John Mark and Jazz. I think they're the ones who found you." I startled at the thought, actually jerking my leg. When she'd said *kids* earlier, I thought she meant someone little.

"They told me to talk to you about Spider-Man, and the state of the universe. The boy, John Mark, told me to hum Beatles tunes for you." She shook her head and laughed. "Which I haven't done. You wouldn't want to hear my humming."

"The other boy?" I asked.

"The other boy came a couple of days ago and left this." Helen held up a book of van Gogh's pictures. "He didn't stick around."

"Todd," I said. A deep nudge in my chest right behind my breastbone left a pain. "Did he say anything else?"

"Nope. Not to me, anyway."

Under the sheet, my hand gouged my thigh, but above the sheet, I was still. *Todd, you are a jerk!* I thought. Those words released some memory. It began at Cherith Rock with him, and then there was the apartment, and then that numbing darkness. I saw van Gogh's eyes.

I was drifting off when the doctor came in. He was a massive man with sandy blond-gray hair. He filled the room like a sheepdog. He was one of the loudest people I'd ever been around.

"How are you feeling now? You look so much better. Is your head still hurting? I'm sure it's better because you are doing well. You'll be able to get around with some crutches, and your right side is looking good."

I jumped in because he was answering all my questions for me. "I am feeling better. A bit of headache."

"Good. We'll be releasing you in a few days. You've made a great recovery." He left as abruptly as he'd come in.

The next day the door opened, and John Mark and Jazz walked in. They sat in the chairs pushed against the wall by the door. I was glad to see them.

"Finally, you are awake," Jazz said. "This is real."

"Yeah," John Mark said, "you had us freaked the last time we were in here."

"Was it you guys who found me? Helen, a nurse's aide, told me some kids found me."

"That was us," John Mark said.

"When I found Spider-Man, I wondered," Jazz said. A piece of paper with a numbered list flashed into my mind. "At first I thought maybe you'd gone away for the weekend. I don't know—with your mom or something."

"But the next morning on my way to work, I found your package in the door," John Mark said. "I opened it during my break and saw that it was your sketchbook." The quotation from the back of the book ran through my mind. The memory of the day before I'd come here was returning. My heart thumped sideways in my chest. Was I excited or afraid? I wasn't sure.

"I wondered why you gave it to me," John Mark said. "I was off by ten, so I called Jazz."

"I told him about Spider-Man, and since that seemed strange to both of us, we decided to go to your place and talk to you," Jazz said.

I looked over to John Mark, because whenever one paused to breathe, the other one picked up. It seemed like they were going back and forth without thinking about it. "And when we got there, your mom answered the door," John Mark said. "She said you weren't home."

"As we added things up, it seemed so final. More like a good-bye for good, not a good-bye for the weekend," Jazz said.

"That scared us," John Mark said.

"We didn't know for sure, but we wondered." Jazz paused, looking down, like she didn't or couldn't put anything more into words.

"About suicide?" I said.

"Yes," Jazz said with a tremendous sigh. "I remembered that you'd made a few comments about it. So John Mark and I just started walking along the tracks."

I found my mind racing along the rails as Jazz talked. I was climbing the rock and looking at the stars. The stars. Light-filled warmth filled me as I remembered the timeless space.

"And we found you and you looked really bad," John Mark said. "And why did you just start smiling?"

"I remember now," I said. "I did go up there to commit suicide, but in the end I didn't. I was throwing the aspirin bottle down the hill when I slipped. And then I was here."

"God, that's freaky," Jazz said. "You wanted to die, then you didn't, then you almost do, but then you don't. How bizarre is that?"

I felt a laugh coming up from deep inside. I couldn't hold it back. The sheer absurdity was phenomenal. It burst out of my mouth with the force of seventeen years. It was an explosion. I couldn't remember the last time I laughed so hard. Jazz and John Mark joined in. Tears splashed, my ribs hurt, and I was gasping. It felt so good to be here with them, to know they had come looking for me.

"You're supposed to be here—that's for sure," John Mark said. "On Earth, not in the hospital, I mean."

"Thanks, guys. For finding me," I said. Jazz was standing beside my bed now, and she touched my arm with her fingertips, carefully avoiding the tubing. "For being there." I didn't expect a response.

John Mark said, "I've got to get going."

"Me too," Jazz said.

They both got up and moved toward the door. As John Mark opened it, he said, "We'll be back."

Seventeen

On Monday Stella walked in, her frosted hair blown back, and her brown vinyl jacket wide open. I turned the television off as her mouth opened.

"You're looking better! Sorry I wasn't around the last couple days, but I moved the first load of stuff up to Merritt."

My mind slowed on hearing Stella's words *I moved.* I blanked out. I was missing something here. Where? When? Did I forget or did I not know?

I tried to go back to the days before Todd and the breakup. She had gone up to Lou's, I did remember that, but I didn't remember specific plans.

Stella frowned and tapped her right foot. "Lou asked me to come live with him, and I haven't had such a good invitation in years. After what's happened here lately, I didn't think you'd want to stay."

I waited for a familiar flood of something, but I had no words. None. I wanted to probe the blankness, the slowness in my mind, but I felt like I was swimming through Jell-O.

"Sorry, Jude." The *tap-tap* of Stella's boot became a squeak as I watched her wiggle it back and forth across the linoleum. "I can see you're shocked. Hell. Like I said, I've never been too good with timing. I thought maybe this would be good news, but maybe it's too much or something." Her voice had gotten quieter on the word *something.*

Shock, yeah, that was it. I was dazed. Were things changing or not changing? I couldn't figure out how I felt.

"I talked to the doctor," Stella went on. "He says they're letting you out of here on Wednesday, so I'll be back then. It's a nice place up in Merritt, Jude. Not too far from the river." I still didn't know what to say, and I didn't want to say anything before I was ready.

"Well," Stella said, "I guess I'll be going." She waved, and I waved back as she left.

I sipped the ice water by the bed. The nurse came in and did the blood pressure, heart rate, temperature stuff. She checked the IVs. She helped me adjust my bed, which meant leg rearranging. The sun was coming across my face now.

Stella hadn't asked me about moving. The thought made me angry, but it didn't consume me. I stared at the dust motes that floated in the sun stream. The anger wasn't a big yawning chasm I had to get across. It was there, real, but it wasn't all of me.

I remembered three bushes: a yellow forsythia, a blue hydrangea, and a pink bush. Spirea—that was the name of it. They were huddled together outside the place where we lived in Memphis, and I had made this great little hiding place under them. It was my own place and I'd loved it. A piece of sadness drifted in as I pictured the bushes, but it became anger. The anger I'd felt when we moved. That was the first time I'd really felt angry. I realized that now.

I hadn't wanted to leave Memphis, but I wasn't sure how I felt about E-ville. I didn't need to stay in E-ville for Todd anymore. There were bad memories in E-ville, but there were some very good ones too. Stella didn't know about them. If I were her, I probably would have come to the same conclusion that she had, that I would want to move on. I wasn't sure how I felt or what I wanted to do next, but this time Stella wouldn't define it for me by what she did. I knew that now. I could choose things for myself. I'd made that decision up on the rock.

I heard a knock; then the door, which was open a little crack, opened up farther and John Mark stuck his head in.

"Come on in now that you're in," I said as he and Jazz walked in.

Words began streaming out of John Mark's mouth like he was a disc jockey: "And now for the news from E-ville High. The Mona Lisa asked about you today. She came to visit you last week, but you were out of it. And since you were gone so long, I realized that you might have missed the news that the football team lost in the state play-offs."

High school? Football? All that seemed like a million years ago. A whole life away. It was hard to picture it.

Jazz said, "Spider-Man is doing great. He's living in my sister's room." They probably fed him lots of canned cat food. I pictured Spider-Man on that star quilt. I was sure he was fat and happy, and I'd never get him back.

They both stopped talking, and I knew they had more questions about what had happened to me. John Mark stared at me with his eyebrow raised, hand on hip. Jazz threw him a glance.

"I guess you guys want to know the whole story of what happened."

"Are you sure you want to talk now?" John Mark said.

Jazz jumped in before I could answer: "I just got to tell you, Jude"—she licked her lips—"it's hot in here." She walked to the window and tried to open it, but it wouldn't budge.

"It's not the greatest story," I said. "Embarrassing even."

"Okay . . ." Jazz said.

"I came here, to E-ville I mean, with so many questions about myself, and my life. I thought my grandmother would give me answers, even *be* an answer, and that things could change. Then she died." I said all that without even pausing for a breath. "And then there's Todd. I had these stupid ideas about him really loving me, taking care of me, and giving me a home." It sounded so dumb as I said it. A flush moved up my face. I closed my eyes. "Penny Lane" went through my head, and I wanted to hum, but I didn't. I went on with my eyes closed.

"But he didn't feel the same way. And we broke up and I felt so alone and stupid." I stopped and looked at Jazz. "I know, I know. You tried to warn me." Jazz put up her hand in a slicing motion that said, *Cut it out.*

"And one night I yelled at this baby I was babysitting, and I just knew I was going to end up like my mother." I stopped. It was a while before I could go on.

"The mind-ache felt terminal, and I was tired of fighting it. The pain was coming out everywhere, and I just wanted to end it. Suddenly I knew why van Gogh had done what he did. He wanted to escape his own life—the inevitability of what he saw in front of him." I paused; it was going to be hard to say the next thing.

Jazz walked over and carefully put an arm on my shoulder. "You don't have to say anything else." Her kindness did it. I felt the tears sliding down my face. Would I be able to stop crying?

"God, Jude," John Mark said. "You are so honest."

I figured I'd better go on quickly, or else I wouldn't. "So it seemed right. In the midst of this long tunnel of pain. I thought I'd use his answer. 'You take death to reach a star.'"

"That's the quote on the back of your notebook," John Mark whispered.

"Yeah. There wasn't supposed to be an accident. I was going to take the aspirin, down the vodka, and lie down on the tracks and wait for the train to come." My voice was shaky. "It was supposed to be the end. You know, death. Sounds better than suicide, doesn't it? Suicide seems small and cheap, and it wasn't going to be that. I thought I was doing the best thing. I was cheating fate."

Jazz squeezed my shoulder. I looked up at her, and there were tears in her eyes. I looked back down at the bed, fighting my own tears again. "But I wanted to say good-bye to the rocky point, the stars. It didn't turn out that way, though. When I got to the highest rock and looked up, the light of the stars came down around me. I didn't go to them."

"What do you mean?" John Mark asked.

"It was transcendent. I was in some sort of cosmic intersection—God, that sounds so made up, but it wasn't. And this place wasn't empty; it was full, and I just knew I wasn't alone." I felt a pain in my arm. I saw that I was clutching my hands, and it was tugging on some tubing, so I let go.

"It was amazing. Things were so much bigger from up there. I don't have it all figured out yet. Then I heard this noise, and saw the train lights coming toward me, and they weren't his eyes anymore. Van Gogh's."

I look at John Mark. His mouth was open. He licked his lips and then swallowed.

"I knew I wanted to live," I said. "And then I went to throw the aspirin bottle away, and my foot slipped. That's the last thing I remember."

"And we found you," John Mark said.

"Yeah."

"I'm glad you didn't want to die," John Mark

said. "God, that sounds so dumb, but you know what I mean."

"No more van Gogh eyes?" Jazz asked.

"No," I answered. "But I can't say that I'll know what to do with all the pain, the sadness. I can't change my history, but I guess I'm not as afraid anymore. I don't know what else to say for now . . ."

"So when are you coming back to school?" John Mark said.

"I don't know," I said. "Stella's moving in with Lou. Up in Merritt."

"That's bad," John Mark said.

"That's Stella," I said.

There didn't seem to be much for them to say to that, so they told me good-bye and walked out. As I watched them walk out the door, I knew that I wanted to stay in E-ville. I had friends I could count on. I pictured the art room, and my fingers could almost feel a paintbrush in them. I thought of poetry class, and the notebook of poems I'd written. As I pulled those things toward me, I knew I wanted to go back to school. I wanted to finish something.

Ms. Dennis came to see me the next day. It was late afternoon. She was carrying a stack of paintings. She lined them up against the wall. It was my chair series.

"I was saving these for you," she said.

"Thanks," I said. "I'm sorry I didn't come to see you that day after school. I just chickened out."

"That's okay, Jude. I should have looked for you. I knew you were in pain. I could see it in your paintings."

"My grandmother died, and there was other stuff." Todd was in the art class. She knew about him. Only a wooden dummy would have missed the vibes. I blushed.

"I want to ask you to forgive me for not coming to you," said Ms. Dennis. "You missed school, and I thought you were sick. Then there was the envelope, and I wasn't sure what it meant until after the accident. By that time it was too late."

For a moment I was speechless. I couldn't remember anyone ever asking me for forgiveness.

I looked down at the sheet and said, "I forgive you." I blundered on: "But to be honest, it was your kindness that scared me away. I didn't know what to do with that."

"Yes, I know. That can be hard to take when you aren't used to it. You'll be finding out more about that in the days to come. We all need kindness."

I looked out the window to hide my tears.

"Jazz told me that your mom is moving."

"She's already started," I said.

"Do you want to go with her?" Ms. Dennis asked. "It is your senior year."

211

"No, I don't."

"I think we can do something about that," Ms. Dennis said. "I talked to Jazz's mom before I came here. She would love to have you stay with them for the rest of the school year. It's up to you."

Had I heard right? It was almost impossible to believe. "But what about Stella?" I asked. As I said it, I realized that I felt some sort of responsibility for her. I'd taken care of her almost as much as she had taken care of me.

"I can talk to her, Jude. I'll let her know you have an option to stay."

"That would be great," I said.

"It's the least I can do, Jude. I wish I could do more. I realize you have a lot to think about. Why don't I call you tomorrow? If you decide to stay with Jazz's family, they could take you home when you're released."

There was no need for me to think about it. I'd made the decision to stay yesterday before I even realized I had options, but I wanted to tell Stella myself and I wanted to hear something from her. We owed it to each other. "Thanks for helping me. Yes, call me tomorrow," I said.

Stella walked into my room Wednesday morning right after they'd brought my breakfast tray. I pulled on my blanket. I felt nervous about telling her how I felt. We didn't communicate on that level too well, and I wasn't sure how she would respond.

She looked at the eggs and said, "I feel better about my attempts at cooking. I can't be any worse."

"That's true," I said.

"You're looking good," she said. Her eyes darted around the room. She saw my paintings. "Are those yours?"

"Yep," I said. "You haven't seen any of my recent stuff. These were inspired by van Gogh, the painter. Ms. Dennis brought them yesterday."

"Oh," Stella said. She looked through the paintings. "I don't know much about him, but it looks like you're trying all sorts of stuff. Looks good to me, but I'm no judge, as you know. You always did like art, though. We moved your box often enough." She smiled at me, and I smiled back.

"That Ms. Dennis called me last night and said that Jazz's family said you could live with them if you want to stay here." She swiped at a piece of hair that had fallen across her face.

"Yeah," I said. "I've decided to stay with them. I want to live here and finish high school."

"You sure?" Stella asked.

"Yes." I stopped because I'd been giving a lot of thought to what I'd say, and I wanted to get it out

213

right, or as best I could. I wanted her to know it was my choice to stay. "This is your move, Stella. Not mine." She flinched but kept looking at me, not taking her eyes from mine. "This time I'm not going with you. I have some really good friends here, and I want to keep working on my art."

"Well, you seem to know what you want." She pulled on the big silver hoop in her ear. "And God knows you are old enough"—she paused, looked at the floor, and then back at me—"and wise enough to make your own decision this time. I wouldn't want to stop you."

"Thanks," I said. We both knew she couldn't have stopped me, and I realized I wouldn't want to stop her either.

"Lou seems nice," I said. I didn't say *compared to the others*. Stella was probably thinking it anyway. "I hope things work out for you."

Stella came to the bed and touched me on the cheek, and then she brushed back the hair from my forehead. "It's a big place. You can join me and Lou if you want too. Anytime."

"I know," I said.

"I've left Lou's number with Jazz's mom. I'll call you and let you know what's going on with us."

"Let me know how the cats are doing," I said.

She smiled and headed for the door. When she got there, she blew a kiss. We both knew it was a real good-bye, and even though I was hopeful about what was to come, I felt tears gathering in my eyes.

I didn't try to hold them back as they slid down my face. I didn't even brush them away. I wondered if a lot of life is like that, sad and hopeful at the same time.

When Ms. Dennis called, I said, "I'd love to stay with Jazz and her family." I couldn't keep the grin from my voice. Spider-Man would be happy too.

"I'll let them know," Ms. Dennis said. "They'll come pick you up after school today."

Later that afternoon, Helen came into the room and helped me get dressed. It was going to take some getting used to with those crutches.

Helen said, "I'm going to miss you. We've spent a lot of time together, you know."

I grinned. "You mean you're going to miss my television and catching up on the soaps."

Helen laughed. "You're too sharp for your own good, Jude."

Then Jazz and her mom came in to get me. They picked up my paintings, and I followed them down the hall, hobbling awkwardly. On the way we passed a Christmas tree. "What day is it?" I asked Jazz.

"December twenty-second," she said.

I couldn't believe I'd been in the hospital that long. "Damn," I said. "I missed my eighteenth birthday."

Jazz laughed. "Girl," she said, "you had one. A big one."

I took a deep breath and we went outside. I turned my face to the sky and let the big wet splotches of snow kiss my face.

ACKNOWLEDGMENTS

This is a partial list as always. Who can thank all those who have influenced us and as a result our writing? That's a lifetime's worth of gratitude. If I forget you, realize that the memory isn't what it used to be.

First and foremost thanks be to God for His unspeakable Gift.

Thanks to TTWM, ACTS, and the Wednesday prayer group, for your prayers and support.

Thanks to the Hershey Medical Center's Outpatient Psychiatric Program way back in March of 1999.

Thanks to Enos Martin, M.D.

Thanks to my family, each and every one. Your love and support have kept me writing through it all.

Thanks to Marshall's friends who gave me feedback and answered lots of questions. I care for all of you.

Thanks to Vincent, for your courage and inspiration.